PRAISE FOR *BEHIND THE MOON*

"Stellar ... A brilliant piece of theatre you don't want to miss!"
—*A View from the Box*

"*Behind the Moon* is tender, heartbreaking theatre. Irani chips
away – moment by moment, metaphor by metaphor, plate
of food by plate of food – until he reaches the molten core of
this dangerous situation and the broken people within it."
—Liam Donovan, *Next*

"Searing tension is the hallmark of Anosh Irani's
Behind the Moon ... The theme of immigration (loss,
hunger, fear) is almost a genre unto itself. But Irani's
play moves it to another level ... sublime script."
—**Dave Rabjohn,** *Our Theatre Voice*

"Intense and captivating."
—*Times Square Chronicles*

"A beautiful, aching play ... that squeezes the heart ... Anosh
Irani slowly reveals each character's story ... at the end of
Behind the Moon we have seen the effects of immigration
on these three men in a play that is funny, heart-squeezing,
multilayered, detailed, and deeply felt. Terrific play."
—**Lynn Slotkin,** *The Slotkin Letter*

"(Rating: ★★★★) ... Filled with symbols and yet rooted
in the problems of the everyday, *Behind the Moon* casts
a long, powerful shadow that is hard to forget."
—**Glenn Sumi,** *So Sumi*

"Irani has written another thought-provoking slice of life ...
Behind the Moon grabs hold of you from the very beginning and
doesn't let go until the startling ending ... The play is a must see."
—**Paula Citron,** *Ludwig Van Toronto*

Also by **ANOSH IRANI**

DRAMA
The Bombay Plays: The Matka King & Bombay Black
Buffoon
The Men in White

FICTION
The Cripple and His Talismans
Dahanu Road
The Parcel
The Song of Kahunsha
Translated from the Gibberish: Seven Stories and One Half Truth

BEHIND THE MOON

A PLAY

ANOSH IRANI

TALONBOOKS

Talonbooks
9259 Shaughnessy Street, Vancouver, British Columbia, Canada V6P 6R4
talonbooks.com

Talonbooks is located on xʷməθkʷəy̓əm, Sḵwx̱wú7mesh, and səlilwətaɬ Lands.

First printing: 2024

Typeset in Minion
Printed and bound in Canada on 100% post-consumer recycled paper

Talonbooks acknowledges the financial support of the Canada Council for
the Arts, the Government of Canada through the Canada Book Fund, and the
Province of British Columbia through the British Columbia Arts Council and the
Book Publishing Tax Credit.

Rights to produce *Behind the Moon*, in whole or in part, in any medium by any
group, amateur or professional, are retained by the author. Interested persons are
requested to contact the author's agent Pam Winter at GGA, 250 The Esplanade,
Suite 304, Toronto, ON, M5A 1J2, Canada, 416-928-0299, pam@ggagency.ca,
ggagency.ca/.

Library and Archives Canada Cataloguing in Publication

Title: Behind the moon : a play / Anosh Irani.
Names: Irani, Anosh, author.
Identifiers: Canadiana 20240376315 | ISBN 9781772016383 (softcover)
Subjects: LCGFT: Drama.
Classification: LCC PS8617.R36 B44 2024 | DDC C812/.6—dc23

PRODUCTION HISTORY

Behind the Moon was first produced from February 21 to March 19, 2023, by Tarragon Theatre in Toronto with the following cast and crew:

AYUB	Ali Kazmi
JALAL	Husein Madhavji
QADIR BHAI	Vik Sahay

Director	Richard Rose
Assistant Director	Deivan Steele
Set and Costume Designer	Michelle Tracey
Set and Costume Design Assistant	Sarah Yuen
Lighting Designer	Jason Hand
Associate Lighting Designer	Echo Zhou
Sound Designer	Thomas Ryder Payne
Fight Director	John Stead
Stage Manager	Meghan Speakman
Apprentice Stage Manager	Kayla Thomas
Sheridan College Work Placement Interns	Emma Burnett and Kayleigh Mundy

CHARACTERS

AYUB, in his thirties.

JALAL, in his late forties. You can tell that he looked good once, but he is now somewhat beaten, tired. His unkempt beard accentuates the fact.

QADIR BHAI, about fifty, with a kindly demeanour.

SETTING

The play is set in the Mughlai Moon, an Indian restaurant in Toronto. The kind of place where you get the best Indian and Pakistani cuisine at 2 a.m. Where cabbies eat after the night shift and drunken youngsters converge after a hard night of clubbing.

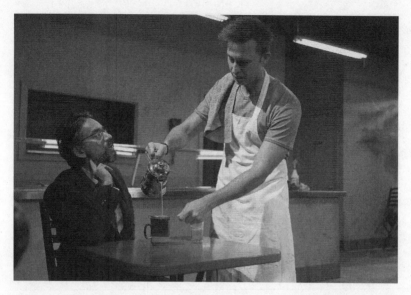

Vik Sahay as Qadir Bhai and Ali Kazmi as Ayub in Tarragon Theatre's production of *Behind the Moon*, photo by Cylla von Tiedemann

Ali Kazmi as Ayub and Husein Madhavji as Jalal in Tarragon Theatre's production of *Behind the Moon*, photo by Cylla von Tiedemann

Husein Madhavji as Jalal, Ali Kazmi as Ayub, and Vik Sahay as Qadir Bhai in Tarragon Theatre's production of *Behind the Moon*, photo by Cylla von Tiedemann

Ali Kazmi as Ayub and Husein Madhavji as Jalal in Tarragon Theatre's production of *Behind the Moon*, photo by Cylla von Tiedemann

ACT 1

SCENE 1

Onstage, a few tables and chairs. A glass display case that is only one-third full of food – dishes that have been kept burning under ugly fluorescent lights all day. It's 3 a.m. The restaurant is now closed. AYUB is by the counter, cleaning the display glass with a cloth, grumbling to himself.

AYUB: Hundreds of times I tell them not to touch the glass. Don't touch, just point.

AYUB sprays some cleaner onto the glass.

But no. They'll touch.

And scrubs again.

What is the need?

He sprays the glass again, with more aggression.

JALAL enters the restaurant. He seems perturbed, very rushed.

(*to JALAL*) Sorry, we're closed.

JALAL doesn't hear AYUB. Or pretends not to. He keeps walking towards the counter.

I said we're closed.

JALAL: Oh.

AYUB: I'm just cleaning up.

JALAL: The door was open, so ...

AYUB shakes his head.

AYUB: I always forget the door ...

AYUB walks past JALAL towards the door and holds it open as a sign for JALAL to leave. But JALAL remains where he is.

JALAL: I just want something quick.

AYUB: Here, everything is quick.

JALAL stares at the food on display.

JALAL: It looks so good.

JALAL looks around the restaurant, a bit manic.

AYUB: No, it doesn't. It used to look good. When I made it. Two days ago.

JALAL: You are the cook?

AYUB: I *was* the cook. Now I'm the cleaner. Here at the Mughlai Moon, we move in and out of multiple roles with great ease. Anyway, I'm sorry, but we're closed.

JALAL: But the food's right there.

AYUB: I know. I'm the one who put it there.

JALAL: Please ... I just finished my night shift.

AYUB: And I'm about to finish mine. Now thank you for visiting this fine establishment.

AYUB makes one spray in the air as a full stop to his statement. Beat.

JALAL: You are from India?

AYUB pretends he didn't hear that.

AYUB: Look, we're closed.

JALAL: It's just that I ... there's this ... I have to sit down.

JALAL sits down in the nearest chair.

I need to sit down –

AYUB: Excuse me, you can't just –

JALAL: I have to. I'm sorry.

AYUB: No, no, get up. You – come on. Get up.

But JALAL doesn't budge.

This isn't ... Fine. You can sit there all you like. But you won't get anything.

JALAL: I normally carry a sandwich with me in the cab. Today, I didn't.

AYUB looks out the window.

AYUB: And I normally carry patience with me. Today, I didn't.

JALAL: Where will I get food at this hour?

AYUB: 7-Eleven, just a block away. Open all night.

JALAL: But I want Indian food. I ... I need Indian food.

AYUB: What do you mean?

JALAL: It *has* to be Indian.

AYUB: Has to be? You make it sound like an emergency.

JALAL: It is.

AYUB: You have an emergency. For Indian food.

JALAL: Right.

AYUB: I've heard of people having an emergency *because* of
Indian food.

> *AYUB indicates his tummy, but JALAL doesn't get it.*

JALAL: Look, I ... anything will do.

AYUB: My cash register's closed. I won't be able to bill you.

JALAL: Bill me tomorrow. Take the money and bill me tomorrow.

> *JALAL frantically checks his pockets for money. His body
> language is getting more desperate.*

AYUB: Hold on. Hold on.

> *JALAL finally finds his wallet.*

I said, hold on.

> *JALAL becomes still. AYUB walks towards JALAL, gets close,
> then stops, examines him.*

Why are you sweating so much?

JALAL: I don't know ...

JALAL checks himself.

Am I?

JALAL wipes his forehead with his sleeve. Realizes that he has been sweating.

AYUB: It's winter.

JALAL: Hah?

AYUB: Why are you sweating in winter?

JALAL: I must have had the heat on too high. In the taxi. I do that sometimes. I start a furnace. Just burn my face. Sorry, this day, it's been … it's the sight of Indian food. The spices trigger the memory. Sweat, watery nose …

AYUB: I see.

AYUB studies JALAL again. Offers him a paper napkin. JALAL wipes his forehead.

JALAL: Thank you.

Beat.

Please. Something. Anything will do.

AYUB: If I were to give you food, what would you choose? I'm not saying that I will – I might not – but if you had to take your pick, what would it be?

JALAL: I … what do you mean?

AYUB: Like I said. If you were to pick something … come. Let me show you what we have.

AYUB leads JALAL closer to the display glass.

JALAL: So you will give me the food?

AYUB: No. I didn't say that. But go near the glass. And choose.
Come, come. Don't worry.

> *AYUB goads JALAL closer, towards the glass, as though he is
> luring a puppy with some treats. JALAL is tentative.*

Now look at what we have here: yesterday's shahi paneer, day
before's lamb korma, yesterday's palak paneer, day before's
mutton biryani, and some murgh masala. I don't know how
old the murgh masala is because it's one of those things that's
always been there, like how you see that homeless fellow outside
and think, "It feels like that guy has always been there." So, for
the murgh masala, I cannot provide a manufacturing date.

> *JALAL scans the food through the glass.*

Come closer.

> *JALAL does. AYUB is watching his every move.*

Come, come. Now choose.

JALAL: Is that ...

AYUB: Which one?

> *JALAL points.*

JALAL: That one. Is it ... butter chicken?

AYUB: Yes, it is. It's very old. The oldest of all. So I didn't even
mention it.

JALAL: Butter chicken ...

> *It's as though JALAL is saying it to himself with some emotion. Then he snaps out of it.*

I will have that.

AYUB: But it's very old.

JALAL: That's okay ...

AYUB: Fine. Is that your final choice?

JALAL: Yes.

> *Beat.*

AYUB: Can you show me which one?

JALAL: I just did.

AYUB: One more time, please. Just to be sure.

> *JALAL points.*

Good. Very good.

JALAL: So you will give me food?

AYUB: Yes. I will. I'll give you food.

JALAL: Oh ... thank you. I don't understand ...

AYUB: Does it matter?

JALAL: No. Thank you.

AYUB goes behind the counter, gets the food, and hands it to JALAL.

How much?

AYUB: Nothing. Cash register closed.

JALAL: No, no, please.

AYUB: The register's closed for the day.

JALAL: You take it then.

AYUB: It's fine. Don't worry about it.

JALAL: No, no, that's not right. Please, I want to –

AYUB: I insist. It's a gift. One dead chicken. Smeared in butter. Way past the best-before date.

JALAL: I really appreciate it.

AYUB: It's okay.

JALAL: My name is Jalal.

JALAL offers his hand. AYUB shakes it. But does not introduce himself.

And you are ...

AYUB: Late. I'm late. I have to go.

JALAL: Oh. In that case, maybe I can give you a cab ride?

AYUB: A cab ride?

JALAL: Yes. To repay you ... for your kindness.

AYUB: Where would we go?

JALAL: I don't know. Anywhere. You said you were late. So maybe I could drop you home?

AYUB: No, I'm good.

JALAL: Array! Koi baat nahi. Koi baat nahi.[1]

AYUB: There's work to be done. Here.

JALAL: I can wait.

AYUB: No. But thank you.

JALAL: It's no problem. I can just sit here and eat while you –

AYUB: That will be all.

JALAL: Oh. Okay. I hope I did not –

AYUB: You didn't.

> AYUB nods. JALAL turns to leave. AYUB goes back to his cleaning. JALAL faces AYUB again.

JALAL: I'm really sorry. But I have to ask.

AYUB: Ask what?

JALAL: Why did you give me the food?

AYUB: You said it was an emergency.

---

1   Hindi: It's not a problem at all.

JALAL: I'm not sure if you believed me.

AYUB: Does it matter?

JALAL: I would be grateful if you told me.

AYUB: Fine. I gave you the food because you passed the test.

JALAL: Test? What test?

AYUB: You did not touch the glass. When you chose your food, you did not touch the glass.

SCENE 2

The next morning. AYUB is at the counter again. He is about to go into the kitchen when QADIR BHAI enters from the main door.

AYUB: Qadir Bhai. Good morning.

QADIR BHAI: Good morning, Ayub. Good morning. How are you?

AYUB: I'm good, Qadir Bhai. Thanks to you, all is good.

AYUB has a different manner when he is with QADIR BHAI. He is respectful. Docile, almost.

QADIR BHAI: Not me. Allah does. We follow. Allah is the doer.

AYUB: Yes, Qadir Bhai. Thanks to Allah, all is good. So, how was Montréal?

QADIR BHAI: God willing, we will open a Mughlai Moon there.

AYUB: Inshallah.

QADIR BHAI: It's not finalized yet. The papers are not signed. These banks say yes and then suddenly they say no.

AYUB: I'm sure the banks will have no issue with you. You already have two Mughlai Moons. One here, one in Vancouver. Two moons. Even our universe has just one.

QADIR BHAI: That's something your baba would have said. You remind me so much of him. Not a day goes by when I don't think of him. May the Almighty grant him eternal peace.

It seems as if AYUB wants to ask QADIR BHAI something but is trying to find the courage. Or the right words.

AYUB: Qadir Bhai, I was wondering ...

QADIR BHAI: Just make sure you keep this place clean.

AYUB: I do. Of course, I do. That's all I do. I mean, that's not all. I cook, too. That is my main task, but –

QADIR BHAI: Your main task has changed. I'm changing it. Now, your main task is to keep the place clean. Cleaner.

AYUB: I ... I don't understand.

QADIR BHAI: Indian Palace just got shut down.

AYUB: What? Why?

QADIR BHAI: Sanitation reasons.

AYUB: I just passed that place three days ago.

QADIR BHAI: The sanitation department shut it down yesterday. Out of nowhere they came.

AYUB: What was the issue?

QADIR BHAI: Rats. They found rats in the restaurant. Not even in the kitchen. Just imagine. In the actual restaurant.

AYUB: How many?

QADIR BHAI: Does it matter? One rat, ten rats? If you must know, they found just one rat. You lead a moral life your whole life and then, just before dying, you commit one big sin. That's your *one* rat.

AYUB: How did you find out?

QADIR BHAI: You know George? The man with the limp? The guy who keeps eating here and saying *their* food is better? He told me. So, you be careful.

AYUB: Of course, of course.

QADIR BHAI: I mean it, bhai. Otherwise, the banks will look the other way.

AYUB nods.

AYUB: Will Indian Palace reopen?

QADIR BHAI: Who knows? Depends on their mood. Banks and sanitation department. So moody.

AYUB: If it doesn't reopen, good for us, no?

QADIR BHAI: No, no. Don't think that way. I don't like Indian Palace. I don't like their food. And I definitely don't like the owner, but he has a wife and kids. They may be our rivals, but where will he go? How will he support them?

AYUB: I'm sorry. I didn't mean ...

QADIR BHAI: Never build a fortune on someone else's misfortune.

AYUB: I'm sorry.

QADIR BHAI: It's okay. When my son says something like that, I gently remind Javed. It all comes back. In the end, every single thought has to be accounted for. So, start the day that way.

QADIR BHAI turns to leave.

AYUB: Qadir Bhai, I ... I would like to discuss something ... I ...

QADIR BHAI: Yes?

AYUB: I would like to go to Mumbai for a visit.

QADIR BHAI: Oh.

AYUB: It will be four years now. Four years since I have seen my
Fatima and –

QADIR BHAI: Ayub, we will speak. We will speak. Once Eid
is done, we will discuss. I promise. After Eid, things will
slow down.

AYUB: But ... I was hoping to celebrate Eid there, with them.
Maybe I can go quickly and come back?

QADIR BHAI: It's India. There is no "quickly." The restaurant has
plans here. Right now, we're expanding. I have found the perfect
location in Montréal. It's just waiting for us. And I will need
your help to set up.

AYUB: Really? That would be perfect. I could move there, Qadir
Bhai. I could manage Montréal for you. I could –

QADIR BHAI: We shall see, Ayub. We shall see. All in good time.

> QADIR BHAI moves towards AYUB and places his hand on
> AYUB's shoulder.

For now, just make sure this place is clean. So clean that if a
customer were to look down, he'd be able to see his own face in
the tiles.

SCENE 3

*A couple of days later. 3 a.m. AYUB is cleaning the glass.
There's a knock on the door. It's JALAL. AYUB opens it, but
does not let him in. He stands by the door.*

JALAL: Kaise hain aap?[2]

AYUB: I'm fine, thank you. You can't keep coming here like this.

JALAL: I just came to tell you that your food was excellent.

AYUB: It can be.

JALAL: It was, it was.

AYUB: No, it was stale. But who am I to argue?

JALAL: And to thank you for your kindness.

AYUB: Sorry?

JALAL: That is also why I came.

AYUB: Okey-dokey.

JALAL: Right ...

AYUB: See? It's confusing, isn't it?

JALAL: What is?

---

2   Urdu: How are you?

AYUB: What is okey? What is dokey? This is the whole problem. With everything. Where does one get clarity nowadays? There's just no clarity.

JALAL: Of course. I just ... I wanted to pay for my food.

JALAL reaches into his pocket and takes out some money.

AYUB: No, no, I told you. Forget about it.

JALAL: I don't want you to think –

AYUB: I'm not thinking anything. You offered me a cab ride home. That might end up costing you more.

JALAL: That is fine with me. My Aida will be happy to take you.

AYUB: Who?

JALAL: Aida.

AYUB: Who is Aida?

JALAL: My taxi. Her name is Aida.

AYUB: You have given your taxi a name?

JALAL: Not just any name, my friend. Aida means "Happy." Or "Helper." My "Happy Helper" at your service.

AYUB: Okay ... Anything else?

JALAL: Shall I point?

AYUB: Hah? Oh. You want food again?

JALAL: Yes, but this time no emergency. Normal hunger.

AYUB: I'm sorry, but I can't. That was the one time ...

JALAL: I understand.

AYUB: Okey-dokey.

JALAL: I will come during normal hours.

AYUB: Good.

JALAL: Another time.

AYUB: You know what? It's okay.

JALAL: Are you sure?

AYUB: Just point.

JALAL smiles. He points to the butter chicken.

Butter chicken, again?

JALAL shrugs.

JALAL: This time, you will accept payment.

AYUB: I can't. After closing, I can't.

JALAL: I am beginning to think that you are tricking me.

AYUB: How's that?

JALAL: Now I will have to give you two taxi rides instead of one.

AYUB: You don't owe me anything.

JALAL: I could always help you clean up. I don't mind.

AYUB: Don't you have a family to go home to?

JALAL: No.

AYUB: What about a TV?

JALAL: Of course.

AYUB: Then go home to your TV.

JALAL: I can help you clean up and then I can drop you home.

AYUB: That's not necessary. I live close by.

JALAL: Are you sure?

AYUB: Sure, sure.

JALAL: Then I will get some food and be on my way.

AYUB: Coming right up. That's what the woman always says.

JALAL: What woman?

AYUB: The waitress. In any English movie, the waitress always says, "Comin' right up."

JALAL: Is that so?

AYUB: She also says, "Will that be all, honey?" But I can't say that. That would be odd.

JALAL: You watch a lot of movies?

AYUB: I used to. When I was little.

JALAL: Is that how you learned English?

AYUB: What do you mean?

JALAL: Nothing. I mean ... your English is so good. You speak –

AYUB: So is yours. But I didn't ask why.

JALAL: I did not mean anything by that.

AYUB: I went to an English school, okay? Maybe it doesn't look like it.

JALAL: No, no, why do you say that? There is no way to look ...

AYUB: Then why'd you bring it up?

> *AYUB realizes he is being sharp.*

I mean ...

> *He hands JALAL his food. Then he indicates his cleaning.*

I have to get back ...

JALAL: Yes, I understand.

> *AYUB starts cleaning the glass again.*

What is this thing between you and the glass?

AYUB: Hah?

> *JALAL imitates AYUB's incessant scrubbing.*

It's my job. To keep it clean.

JALAL: You feel very strongly about it.

AYUB: I take pride in my work. Don't you keep your taxi clean?

JALAL: But I keep the *entire* taxi clean. I don't spend all day cleaning the windshield.

AYUB: Are you saying that the rest of this place is dirty?

JALAL: No, I'm not. I'm just saying. I am … interested.

AYUB hesitates.

AYUB: Fine. I see hundreds of people every week. Sometimes the same people, over and over. The other day this woman comes in. She's Indian, kind of pretty, pretty like a colour that's faded. I had this T-shirt when I was little, and I wore it all the time, it was this strange blue colour – and over time it faded, because of the constant washing.

AYUB stops abruptly.

Anyway. See you around.

JALAL: What do you mean?

AYUB: I have to work.

JALAL: What about the T-shirt?

AYUB: What about it?

JALAL: The T-shirt, the woman?

AYUB: She used to be pretty once, like the T-shirt. But *used to be* is very different from *is*, and it's not that looks matter, but it was her general attitude, that made me, how shall I say, not warm up to her. I still kept an open mind, but the more she looked at the food and the menu and then at me, I realized she was one of those Indians who thinks she's better than some other Indians, and I could also tell that she wasn't too happy about eating here, in this establishment, it was something circumstances had forced her to do, and I knew, I just knew, that she was one of those people who would touch the glass.

JALAL: Did she?

AYUB: Did she? Of course she did. She touched the glass. Not only did she touch the glass, she placed her entire palm on it, like this.

JALAL: Wow.

AYUB: Exactly.

JALAL: So what did you do?

AYUB: I, very nicely, with the charm and grace of someone who is in the hospitality business, told her, "Please don't put your palm on the glass." And that's when she told me to fuck off. So, I smiled. I smiled not because I enjoy being abused, but because it only proved my theory about her. But the smile made her more angry, and she asked for the owner, and so I went and got Qadir Bhai, and long story short, Qadir Bhai made me apologize to her.

JALAL: He made *you* apologize?

AYUB: The customer is always right.

JALAL: Is that so?

AYUB: It's the law of the jungle.

JALAL: So, as a customer, no matter what I do, I'm right?

AYUB: Correct.

JALAL: So if I touched the glass right now, placed my entire palm over it, you would have to apologize to me?

AYUB: Yes, I would. For cutting off your fingers. You see, right now the place is closed, and you are not a customer.

JALAL: Ah. Good point.

AYUB: I think it's an excellent point.

JALAL: Sometimes I cannot tell if you are joking or serious.

AYUB: Neither can I. I only find out after the fact. I'll say something, and then I'll let it hang in the air for a while. And only then will I know if I was serious or if what I said had some ... some levity to it. Like even this thing I'm saying right now, about levity, am I being funny or am I being ... something else? How do I know? I let it hang.

   AYUB lets it hang.

JALAL: Are you okay?

AYUB: Of course. Why wouldn't I be?

JALAL: You seem a bit worried.

AYUB: I'm not worried.

JALAL: Not worried. How do they say it? On edge.

AYUB: There's just no clarity anymore. People say one thing, but they mean something else. Or do they mean exactly what they say?

JALAL: I don't know.

AYUB: See? No clarity.

JALAL: It all depends on the person. Some people mean what they say. Others don't.

AYUB: But sometimes it's hard to tell the difference! It's okay, it's all part and parcel ...

JALAL: Of what?

AYUB: Nothing. All good.

JALAL: Look, if you need some help, I –

AYUB: Help?

JALAL: Yes, you seem upset.

AYUB: People are upset all the time.

JALAL: I'm just saying. Kya main aapke liye kuch kar sakta hoon?[3] You speak Urdu?

AYUB: Look, we're not friends, okay?

JALAL: I understand. I'm just trying to –

AYUB: I just gave you food, that's all.

JALAL: And I'm just trying to return the favour.

AYUB: There's nothing wrong with me.

---

3   Urdu: Is there something I can do for you?

JALAL: I didn't say there was.

AYUB: But you think, don't you?

JALAL: I did not mean any offence. I just want you to know that I'm grateful for what you did for me.

AYUB: I just gave you food! It's not a big deal.

JALAL: It was. (*beat*) Forget about it. I should go.

AYUB: Okay.

JALAL: It's just that … I go wherever Aida takes me. When there's a passenger, it's different. She remains silent. She has to. She lets me do my job. But when we are alone, it's as though she does the driving. Sometimes, she takes me places. That night, she brought me here, to you. I was saying to her, "Aida, please guide me. Tell me what to do." And then, I saw this place. What I'm saying is, what I'm trying to say is, maybe it is destined.

AYUB: What is?

JALAL: Us. What if we are destined to meet? The two of us.

AYUB: To what end?

JALAL: There is no end. That is exactly my point. *Her* point. Every day I ask her, "Why? Why? What's the point? What's the point to it all?" And those are the times she remains silent. And then a drunk couple will enter the cab and fill the space with their … their vulgar breath. And I bless them, I bless them for being there, with all their cash and full lips, and the way they speak about their friends, the very friends they were just with, and then I realize that they are not even husband–wife, it is someone else's husband with someone else's wife, and they are sticking their tongues

— 30 —

down each other's throats *because* of that, as though if they stick their tongues deep enough, long enough, they will taste something ... truthful for once, find the answer to why they are doing this, and that is when I want to laugh, I want to tell them I am a step ahead, life has not caught up with them as yet, it is sniggering in the corner, it is just round the bend, waiting for them ... but they have no clue. And when I take their money, I smile, and they think I am being courteous, but I'm doing it out of compassion, maybe I am anticipating the pain that is about to come their way, I don't know. But I want to say to them that when they open that door and step onto the curb ... life is waiting.

JALAL moves closer to AYUB.

Aida is not just any vehicle. She is a vehicle for the truth. And the truth is that when I walk through that door ...

JALAL turns to the exit.

... I know it is a door that opens ... into nothing.

JALAL exits. AYUB watches him leave. He tries to get back to his cleaning. But he's disturbed. He sprays some liquid in the air. A single spray. Not satisfied, he sprays some more, in the direction of the main door, as though he is trying to clear the memory of Jalal, and of what he just said.

SCENE 4

Morning. The restaurant is empty. QADIR BHAI enters, staring at his phone as though he is expecting an important call. His walk is extremely buoyant. He starts talking but does not notice that AYUB isn't even there.

QADIR BHAI: How many moons does this universe have? Hah? Can you tell me?

AYUB pops his head up from below the counter.

AYUB: One?

QADIR BHAI: And what was it you said the other day? That I have two? Isn't that what you said?

AYUB: That's what I said.

QADIR BHAI: Well, you were wrong. I am now the proud owner of three moons! One-two-three!

AYUB: The bank approved?

QADIR BHAI: And how! But it's not the banks. It's not the banks!

QADIR BHAI looks up.

Allah approves. All approvals come from Allah.

AYUB: Allah is merciful.

QADIR BHAI: Merciful and how!

AYUB nods.

A Mughlai Moon in Montréal. They speak French there. They use words like "petit" and "Monsieur." Do you know what that means? It means "small" and "Mister." I was a small man, a man who came from nothing, and I am now a Monsieur. My lawyer said that to me over the phone, "It's all done, Monsieur Qadir." I almost fell off my stool. I was in the kitchen, cutting vegetables for my wife. And I wanted to tell her, "You are making Monsieur Qadir cut vegetables?" And the lawyer pronounced my name not Qadir but Ka-Deer. The man made me a deer. How elegant are the French? He just ... just transformed me from something ordinary to ... to a deer. Have you ever seen a deer? It is the most graceful of creatures ... I came from nothing, Ayub. That's what makes this country so great. You can come from nothing and *become*. If you just keep your head down and work hard, you can become a Monsieur. No, what am I saying – a deer!

AYUB: Yes, Qadir Bhai. I keep my head down. I do. And I work hard.

QADIR BHAI: I know you do. I know how hard you work.

AYUB: It's just that ... it's hard to –

QADIR BHAI: I know, Ayub. I know. It is hard. You feel alone. I understand that. When I first came here ... I had no one. Absolutely no one. I worked in construction, Ayub. It was hard, hard work. And it was fine. But ... during the lunch break, no one would eat lunch with me. I sat alone. All alone. Every single lunch. They even made fun of the way I talked. So I did not talk at all. I just worked and worked.

AYUB: I'm sorry to hear that ...

QADIR BHAI: Don't feel sorry for me! It made me who I am. Now look how much I talk! But ... that taught me something. It taught me to make people feel ... included. To understand where they come from. Their needs. I understand your need, Ayub. And to show that I do, I want to do something for you.

AYUB: Oh.

QADIR BHAI: Don't be so surprised. It's my duty. One must always share one's good fortune. I mentioned this to Javed last night, and even he said, "We must do something for Ayub." And it was his idea, mind you, *he* asked me, "What does Ayub want? What would make him happy?" Now I'm aware that you and Javed ... I understand what you might think of him –

AYUB: Nothing like that, I've never said anything about –

QADIR BHAI: It's okay, it's okay, you don't need to. I understand. He's young, and I know that I have given him too much; not too much but a little more than he deserves, maybe. But we all deserve good things in life, don't we? It's just that I don't want him to go through what I did in this country. I want to protect him, I want to give him the platform that I never had, and he has done so well in university, he will become a lawyer, a man who brings justice, just imagine, a lawyer – he has that *just* streak in him, a need for truth, who knows what he has ... I am a simple man compared to my son. His intelligence is of this country, it's new and has a certain sophistication to it, whereas I am just someone who had to go through the worst of times. But I won't let that happen to my son. And I won't let that happen to you, either. Not after everything your baba did for me. He was ... you know how he was. I don't have to tell you. And I kept my word to him. Didn't I?

AYUB: Yes, you did.

QADIR BHAI: That's right. First chance I got, I brought you here. At great expense to me, mind you. But so what? You are a younger brother to me. Brothers help each other.

AYUB: Thank you, Qadir Bhai. That means a lot.

QADIR BHAI: Don't thank me yet. Thank me one day when you're a big man. And you will be, Ayub. You will be. (*beat*) But – what was I saying? Ah, yes. "What does Ayub want? What would make him happy?" Javed's words, not mine. In that instant, I knew, I just knew, what had to be done. I hope you will be excited by this. I certainly am.

> *AYUB's face does show excitement, a rare happiness.*

You want so badly to see your wife and child, don't you? What else can a man want, a true man, a family man – but to see the two loves of his life?

> *The happiness in AYUB is rising.*

And so ...

> *QADIR BHAI reaches into his jacket and takes out a small package.*

... here you are ... go ahead, open it.

> *As he accepts it, AYUB puts his hand on his chest out of respect and gratitude.*

AYUB: Qadir Bhai ...

QADIR BHAI: Open it, open it ...

> *AYUB slowly opens the package as though he is opening his very future.*

An iPhone! Just for you. You may not be able to go to meet your wife and child, but you can bring them here! You can see them and chat with them as if they are right here!

AYUB is speechless.

This is all Javed, mind you. It was his idea. I said, "Where will we get a phone just now, so late at night? I want to do this fast because he wants to, *needs* to, be with them," and Javed said, "Just give him my phone. Here." This is Javed's phone – he wants a new one anyway – but this one's all yours, so you can throw away that old phone, throw it away! There are good days ahead, Ayub. Good days ahead. What do you say?

AYUB: I ...

QADIR BHAI's phone rings.

QADIR BHAI: It's the lawyer, the French lawyer. (*into the phone*) Hello, Jacques ... yes, Jacques. Monsieur Qadir here!

QADIR BHAI laughs into the phone, light as a feather, dancing on air, and leaves AYUB feeling heavy – lost and confused, with a used iPhone in his hand.

Jacques, can you please hold for a second? (*softly, to AYUB*) I can't see my face, Ayub. In the tiles. I still can't see my face. (*into the phone*) Sorry, Jacques. Just tending to business ... (*whispering to AYUB*) I need to see my face ...

AYUB puts the phone into his pocket, goes to a small door, and disappears down the stairs.

(*into the phone*) La Lune Mughlai! Oh, absolutely. Oui! Oui! (*beat*) The beginning of a great partnership indeed! Who knows where we will go next? Someplace exotic. I mean, what about France itself? Why settle for Montréal? I mean, we're not settling. Montréal is Montréal! (*beat*) Do you have any contacts in Paris? Oui? Wow!

AYUB comes back with some cleaning materials.

(*aside to AYUB, softly but supercharged, covering the phone*)
He has contacts in Paris!

AYUB nods, gets down on his hands and knees, and starts scrubbing the tiles.

SCENE 5

A week later. Night. AYUB is on his hands and knees scrubbing the tiles. He hears a knock. He looks up. AYUB opens the door for JALAL, then immediately goes back to his scrubbing. He speaks to JALAL without looking up. JALAL is holding a thick, cylindrical package in his hand.

AYUB: Haven't seen you in a while.

JALAL: Yes, well ...

AYUB: I thought maybe you'd found another restaurant.

JALAL: No, no. I don't come this way much ...

AYUB: I'd hate to lose a client. Even one as annoying as you. Not that I'm emotional about you. It affects my bonus. (*muttering to himself*) When I do manage to get one.

JALAL: As you can see, I am here.

AYUB: Give me a second. I'm almost done.

JALAL: I do not want any food today.

AYUB: Oh.

JALAL: It was my day off. I ate early. But then I could not sleep. So I thought to myself, "I know someone who'll be awake at this time." (*beat*) I would like to take you somewhere.

AYUB: Take me somewhere?

JALAL: Yes. For a meal. Dinner. (*looking at his watch*) Or a very early breakfast.

AYUB: Not tonight. There's a lot of work to do.

JALAL: I thought you were almost done.

AYUB: You sure you don't want any food?

JALAL: I'm sure.

AYUB: Maybe for tomorrow? You want to keep it in the fridge?

JALAL: Actually ... I want to give *you* something. I got something for you.

> JALAL presents the package to AYUB.

AYUB: What's that?

JALAL: A gift.

AYUB: A gift?

JALAL: Yes.

AYUB: Thanks, but I just got one the other day.

JALAL: Got what?

AYUB: A gift.

JALAL: But ... this one is different. Not all gifts are the same.

AYUB: What if they are?

JALAL: What do you mean?

AYUB: Never mind.

JALAL: Don't you want to know what it is?

AYUB: Sometimes it's better not to know. Sometimes the opening of the gift is the moment when the gift ... you know.

JALAL: No, I don't.

AYUB: It becomes something else.

JALAL: Will you please stop that?

AYUB: My owner wants to see his face in the tiles.

JALAL: What?

AYUB: I can't stop until my owner sees his face in the tiles.

JALAL: Why do you keep saying that?

AYUB: That's what he wants.

JALAL: No, not that. You said, "My owner."

AYUB: Did I?

JALAL: Twice. Even the other day.

AYUB: So?

JALAL: Why would you call him your owner?

AYUB: He's the owner of the restaurant.

JALAL: What's going on here?

AYUB: Nothing's going on. I'm just polishing the tiles.

JALAL: Look, you can talk to me.

AYUB: About what?

JALAL: About anything. You and I, we are –

AYUB: Sure.

JALAL: You can trust me.

AYUB: Why would I trust you? Why would I trust anybody?

JALAL: I'm just saying – look, I know this place can get to you.
I know moving here can be hard.

AYUB: You know nothing of my move.

JALAL: Come on. I too moved from India. I'm from Kashmir.

AYUB: You're an immigrant, so what?

JALAL: We all have something in common. We –

AYUB: No, we don't. You drive a cab. You and I don't have
anything in common.

JALAL: What does that mean?

AYUB: Why are you here? Why do you keep coming here?

JALAL: Are you saying I'm less of a person because I drive a taxi?
I was ... I was doing something else in Kashmir, okay? I was ...
how should it matter?

AYUB: It doesn't. That's what I'm saying.

JALAL: You make it sound like it does.

AYUB: It's these nights.

AYUB is frantic. He presses his temples.

The thoughts come at night. That's when they come for you.
They always come at night. They just –

JALAL: Hey, it's okay.

AYUB: It's like they just …

JALAL: It's okay …

AYUB: What's that?

AYUB listens for something.

What's that sound?

JALAL: What sound?

AYUB: That rumbling. Can you hear it?

But JALAL can't hear anything. AYUB listens to it again.

Never mind …

JALAL: I just … I want to give you something.

AYUB: What are you doing here? What do you want from me?

JALAL: Nothing. If you will just accept this … here, let me open it
for you.

AYUB: No.

JALAL opens his gift.

No, don't do that.

JALAL: It's nothing, you'll see.

AYUB: I said no.

> *But JALAL doesn't wait. He unfurls his gift. It's a small carpet.*

JALAL: It's a carpet. For your wall.

AYUB: Which wall?

JALAL: Any wall. It's a wall carpet. I'll help you hang it up.

> *AYUB looks around.*

Not here. In your home. It's got an inscription ... see here? These threads ... an inscription.

AYUB: What does it say?

JALAL: I will explain when I hang it up. Trust me.

AYUB: Stop saying that.

JALAL: Let me take you home.

AYUB: I don't want your carpet.

JALAL: It's not a carpet.

> *JALAL places the carpet on the floor.*

You were right.

AYUB: About what?

JALAL: About it being something else.

AYUB: I don't want it to become something else.

JALAL: It's too late for that. Let me take you home.

AYUB: I want you to leave.

JALAL: I have to stay. I *know* I have to stay.

AYUB: I don't want to hurt you.

JALAL: Hurt me? Why would you?

AYUB: Just leave me alone.

JALAL: Let me take you home. If you will just sit in my taxi, things will be okay.

AYUB: Tell me, who sent you?

JALAL: What? No one.

AYUB: I'll call the cops.

JALAL: Then call.

AYUB: I'm serious. I will.

JALAL: I have nothing to hide.

> *AYUB picks up the phone. JALAL is cool. AYUB doesn't dial.*

AYUB: I just want to go home. That's all. I just …

JALAL: Let me take you home. That's all I have been saying.

AYUB: I don't want to go home. I want to go home ... but not ...

JALAL: I can drive us.

AYUB: I can walk.

JALAL: Why won't you sit in my taxi?

AYUB: I don't need to!

JALAL: Let me just drive you home.

AYUB: Will you just leave me alone?

JALAL: Something tells me not to. Something is wrong.

AYUB: Stop saying that! Nothing's wrong. I'm fine. It's my choice, okay?

JALAL: What choice?

AYUB: Look, man. Just ...

JALAL scans the restaurant. He looks towards the kitchen.

JALAL: What's back there?

AYUB: Nothing.

JALAL: There has to be something.

AYUB: The kitchen.

JALAL: What's behind *that* door?

AYUB: Whatever's *supposed* to be behind doors. It doesn't matter. There are stairs, okay? There are stairs that lead to a washroom. What else would there be?

JALAL: Fine.

AYUB: Fine.

JALAL: I should go then.

AYUB: Yes. You should. You must.

> *AYUB walks to the main door and opens it for JALAL. But JALAL suddenly turns and dashes towards the door that leads downstairs to the basement.*

No! No, man! Hey!

> *But JALAL is too quick. AYUB rushes down the stairs behind him. They are now both offstage.*

JALAL: (*offstage*) What's that door?

AYUB: (*offstage*) The washroom!

JALAL: (*offstage*) No, the other one.

AYUB: (*offstage*) Will you stop? (*beat*) No, don't!

> *We hear another door open.*

JALAL: (*offstage*) What's this?

AYUB: (*offstage*) Cleaning supplies, man! There's a closet. You want some cleaning supplies? Hah? Is that it? Butter chicken plus supplies? Now, please! Let me get back to work!

JALAL: (*offstage*) Why is there a mattress here? Are these your clothes?

AYUB: (*offstage*) You can't be here. If my owner sees …

JALAL: (*offstage*) He is *not* your owner.

AYUB: (*offstage*) You've seen it, okay? Now please leave. Let's go back up.

JALAL: (*offstage*) You live here?

AYUB: (*offstage*) So what? I … it's temporary.

JALAL: (*offstage*) How long have you lived here?

AYUB: (*offstage*) It's not your business, man!

JALAL: (*offstage*) How do you even breathe in this place?

AYUB: (*offstage*) I breathe just fine.

JALAL: (*offstage*) Are you getting paid?

AYUB: (*offstage*) I get paid. Now please, please … up.

Beat.

JALAL: (*offstage*) But you call him your owner, that man.

The sound of them coming up the stairs.

AYUB: (*offstage*) He owns the place.

JALAL: (*offstage*) You live alone?

AYUB: (*offstage*) Yes … of course …

AYUB and JALAL are now onstage.

JALAL: Do you have someone? Somewhere?

AYUB: How does it matter?

JALAL: Do you have a family?

AYUB: One child. A piece of my heart. A daughter.

JALAL: This makes sense.

> *JALAL seems to be figuring something out in his mind. Then he gets strangely euphoric. AYUB is distressed, exposed.*

This makes sense. It is all making sense. Her name?

AYUB: (*in a voice heavy with shame, defeated*) Ghazal. And my wife's name is Fatima.

JALAL: (*almost as if invoking their names*) Ghazal. Fatima.

AYUB: Don't say their names. You have no right to say their names.

> *JALAL points to the carpet again.*

JALAL: It all makes sense now.

AYUB: I don't want it.

JALAL: Lqd trknā klw šīʾ waraʾana, wa-madayna; fmā kān muqaddaran lnā, qd taḥaqqaqa. Lqd intahaynā, wa-ṣārat aʿmālnā ḥikāyāt tuḥkā li-l-aṭfāl.[4]

---

4   Arabic: We left it all behind, and off we went; what was fated, came to pass. We were done, and our doings became tales for the children.

The quote has a strange effect on AYUB.

AYUB: What is that?

JALAL: The inscription on the carpet.

AYUB: Is that a spell?

JALAL: A spell? No, I just told you. What is inscribed on the carpet.

AYUB: What does it say?

JALAL: Lqd trknā klw šï' wara'ana –[5]

AYUB: In English. Tell me in English.

JALAL: I know, I know.

JALAL translates.

"We left it all behind, and off we went; what was fated, came to pass. We were done, and our doings became tales for the children."

AYUB: What was fated?

JALAL: I ... I must go now.

AYUB: What will become of my child? Tell me what you mean.

JALAL: I must go. I have to go.

AYUB: Who are you?

---

5 Arabic: We left it all behind –

JALAL walks away. AYUB grabs him by the collar.

Tell me!

JALAL: I ... what can I say ... (*pointing*) You see that tree?

> *AYUB stares out the window. JALAL's gaze is that of both reverence and terror.*

See how it shakes? It is trembling.

AYUB: It's windy tonight.

JALAL: No. It has nothing to do with the wind. That tree is shaking because of me. I am the one who makes the trees shake.

AYUB: What do you mean?

> *But JALAL leaves. AYUB is scared. He locks the door. Double checks it to make sure. He stays there, at the door.*

Fatima ...

> *He takes out his iPhone.*

Ghazal ...

Are you okay?

> *But he cannot bring himself to dial. He puts the phone away.*

I can't call you, Fatima.

When I see your face, in it I see my mistakes. And now Qadir Bhai has given me a phone. As though he *wants* me to see your face. And then there is this man … he will not leave me alone. There is evil here …

… in this place, there is evil …

Don't bring her here, Fatima. We can't bring her here. Ghazal, my child, stay there. Please. Here, it snows.

Let me tell you, there is nothing … there is nothing good about snow.

It falls at night, when I am most alone. It is so silent in its judgment, so … gentle in its assault. It is a carpet …

AYUB holds the carpet.

Yes, a carpet … a carpet of my mistakes.

I hope you never see snow, Ghazal. It's not for us … Snow is best seen in your dreams.

I did what you said, Ghazal. When the first snow fell, I went out and did like you told me. I opened my mouth wide, and let it fall in … and the thing is, when I tasted it … it was the ugliest taste … it is not my taste, it is not our taste, it is theirs … it belongs to them. It should never land on our tongue.

I will call you soon, Ghazal. I promise. Your father will call. Fatima, your husband will call.

But … I have to find him first. That man, who is your husband …

AYUB stares at himself in the glass.

I cannot see him.

I'm doing as you said. I'm cleaning the glass. I'm cleaning the glass. But I just cannot see him.

Then he slides his hands against the glass door, placing his entire palms on it, dirtying it immeasurably.

Fatima … Fatima …

With deep yearning, as though someone at the other end of the world can actually hear him, AYUB calls out his wife's name.

Fatima!

He waits for an answer, but there is none.

Fatima!

Dead silence. Eerie.

Please. Someone … answer me. Answer me.

Nothing. Nothing at all.

But then he hears something. We cannot. AYUB turns around. His entire being is filled with horror. Something seems to be coming for him.

Get away from me …

You're not welcome here …

Who sent you? Did Indian Palace send you? Hah?

Get away from me, you dirty …

Go away!

But the dark shadow of something is coming for him.

AYUB falls to his knees. A crumbling mess.

Go away ...

He begs.

Please ...

End of Act 1

ACT 2

SCENE 1

The next day. Noon. AYUB is holding a broom in one hand.
He has a piece of chocolate in his other hand.

AYUB: Let's try some chocolate. No one can resist chocolate, right?

My Ghazal loves chocolate. Little girls, when they eat chocolate, they become demonic. Angel to demon in a matter of seconds.

Look at me. Here I am, talking to you. A rat. Look, it's nothing personal. I have to do this. You have the power to shut us down, so ... no hard feelings.

If my friends saw me now, how they would laugh. They would laugh, then they would look the other way. In shame. "Who told him to leave?"

I don't have a single friend here. Not one. No *buddies*.

Hey, you want to be my Canadian *buddy*? Hah?

Come on out, buddy. Come out so I can ...

Just then the door opens. It's QADIR BHAI. AYUB freezes.
QADIR BHAI has a big black garbage bag in his hand.

Qadir Bhai!

AYUB realizes he is being especially loud. So does
QADIR BHAI.

Good morning ...

QADIR BHAI: Good morning. You seem to have a lot of energy today.

AYUB: Yes, I do. I ... yes, I do. Maybe it's this chocolate.

AYUB eats the piece of chocolate.

All this chocolate ...

QADIR BHAI: But you look tired. You look like a man who hasn't slept all night.

AYUB: I haven't ...

QADIR BHAI: Oh? Is something wrong?

AYUB: No, no. All is well.

But QADIR BHAI's silence is an inquiring one.

It's just that I was ... I was talking with Fatima all night. The phone you gave me, it's ... thank you. Thank you for the phone.

QADIR BHAI: And how is Fatima?

AYUB: She is well.

QADIR BHAI: Did it not fill your heart up to see her?

AYUB: Oh, yes. She looks more beautiful than ever.

QADIR BHAI: That's the thing about a woman. You find the right woman, and she will look better and better.

AYUB: How come you are here, Qadir Bhai?

QADIR BHAI: Does a man need permission to come to his own restaurant?

AYUB: No, no, not at all. It's just that you never come on Sundays.

QADIR BHAI: Then there must be a reason for my visit.

AYUB: Yes, of course. But you don't need a reason. You are always welcome here.

QADIR BHAI: I know that. It's my place. What is wrong with you today?

AYUB: Nothing. I have a bad headache, that's all.

QADIR BHAI: Then take a pill.

AYUB: Yes, yes ...

QADIR BHAI: I need you fit! And well!

AYUB: Yes, of course ...

QADIR BHAI: And stop eating chocolate. Chocolate is bad for your headache!

AYUB: Yes, I'm sorry. I didn't realize ... what can I do for you?

QADIR BHAI: My son is engaged!

AYUB: Engaged? Javed?

QADIR BHAI: Who else? He's the only son I have.

AYUB: Congratulations, Qadir Bhai.

QADIR BHAI: When Allah gives, he gives ... manifold.

AYUB: Qadir Bhai, forgive me for saying this ... but you don't seem very happy.

QADIR BHAI: We haven't met her, Ayub. We haven't even met the girl!

AYUB: Oh.

QADIR BHAI: "Oh" is right. But – I believe that whatever comes our way is sent from above. And if it is sent from above, it can only be good.

AYUB: Even if it's not good?

> *QADIR BHAI is taken aback by this remark. So is AYUB. It just burst out of him.*

I'm sorry, I did not mean it that way.

QADIR BHAI: Care to explain that remark?

AYUB: No, no, it was nothing. It's this headache ...

QADIR BHAI: Still, try and explain yourself.

AYUB: I meant ... I was talking about myself. Sometimes I don't understand what comes my way. I cannot make sense of it.

QADIR BHAI: You don't need to. If it's in front of us, it's meant for us. This girl, Javed's fiancée, is meant for us. Good or bad is irrelevant.

AYUB: I understand.

QADIR BHAI: I don't think you do.

AYUB: I do, I do.

QADIR BHAI: Your lips are just a part of your face, Ayub. Your lips are saying one thing, but your entire face is a big question mark.

Don't question so much. Let things happen as they will. As they must. Certain things *must* happen.

> *AYUB nods.*

AYUB: Where is the girl from? Is she ... Muslim?

QADIR BHAI: Does it matter?

AYUB: No. If it's Javed's choice, then no. It does not matter.

QADIR BHAI: (*with a tinge of disappointment*) She's from here.

Her name is Cindy.

AYUB: Cindy?

QADIR BHAI: Cindy Smith.

AYUB: Cindy Smith ...

QADIR BHAI: Must you keep repeating everything I say? No point repeating it. It will not make it any less certain. Cindy Smith is here. Therefore, I take it that Cindy Smith is meant to happen. Cindy Smith must happen.

Javed, in all his infinite wisdom, the scant wisdom of a boy in love, after proposing to Cindy Smith last night and giving her a big fat ring, invited her and her parents to our home tonight. Tonight. Can you imagine? What was the rush? I asked him. And he just looked at me like this ...

> *QADIR BHAI imitates Javed. A boy dumbfounded like a frozen cartoon character.*

What will he do when he starts practising law? When the judge asks him for his opening statement, will he stand like this?

QADIR BHAI imitates Javed again.

That big fat ring was bought with *my* money. On *his* card, but
he has no money to pay it off. My wife was appalled when she
saw the ring. She said it looked like a tumour. An expensive
tumour. Did you give Fatima a big fat ring? No. I'm sure
you didn't.

AYUB: I didn't give Fatima any ring. I didn't have the money.

QADIR BHAI: Neither does Javed! I have to calm down. The boy
is making my blood pressure rise. But what to do – he's my son.
And we will do anything for our children, won't we? You are a
father. You understand.

AYUB: I tied a string on her finger.

QADIR BHAI: A string? What string?

AYUB: Instead of a ring, I tied a string.

QADIR BHAI: What sort of man ties a string on his wife's finger?

AYUB: A poor man.

QADIR BHAI: And she said nothing? She accepted this *string*?

AYUB: It made her smile.

QADIR BHAI: Your Fatima is an angel. Only an angel would smile
when presented with a string.

AYUB: She was smiling because of what was attached to the string.
At the other end of the string was a kite.

QADIR BHAI: A kite?

AYUB: High up in the sky. A big, yellow kite. I had been flying it, and when she came next to me, I tied it to her finger and said, "Fatima, I am that kite. I have nothing to offer you, except my loyalty. I shall always be tied to you. No matter what. All you have to do is twirl your finger, and I shall move. This way and that, up and down, sideways, anyways. I want to marry you, Fatima. I'm going home, and from my terrace, if I still see the kite, it means you will have me. If not, then cut me loose." Then I ran away. And a few minutes later, I saw that I was still flying high.

QADIR BHAI: Do you want me to fly a kite, Ayub? What are you saying?

AYUB: I'm saying ... that maybe you should trust Javed. Trust that –

QADIR BHAI: Trust Javed? That's interesting. I mean sure, he's my son, but he's also ... an idiot. He's been through nothing. Can you trust someone who's been through nothing?

AYUB: They will find their way, just as Fatima and I did. Love does that. Doesn't it?

   Beat.

QADIR BHAI: You have given me strength today. You have convinced me. Cindy Smith is meant to happen. And her parents, Bob and Sheryl. Bryan and Charlotte? No, Bruce and ... these names are so confusing, so ... forgettable. Mr. and Mrs. Smith. That's enough for now. Cindy Smith. Mr. and Mrs. Smith. You will cook the meal of your life. We will welcome them into our home in the most *delicious* manner.

AYUB: Me?

QADIR BHAI: Who else? You're one of the best chefs I know.

AYUB: Oh. Absolutely, I will. I will make Cindy Smith fall in love, double love, with Javed. Food does that. You share a tasty meal with someone, and you will share a tasty life. My food will do that.

QADIR BHAI: I trust your food. How long will you need?

AYUB: About two, three hours.

QADIR BHAI: Then be at my house by three.

AYUB: I will, I will.

QADIR BHAI: Good. Good. Now. This is for you.

QADIR BHAI raises the black plastic bag.

AYUB: Sure, I will throw it out.

AYUB reaches for it.

QADIR BHAI: Why would you throw it out?

AYUB: It's garbage ... isn't it?

QADIR BHAI: Garbage? I come bearing gifts. These are some of Javed's old clothes. He has sent them for you. I tell you he is getting more and more generous, that boy. Maybe it's the whole in-love thing? But some of these clothes ... I bought them for him. There's an Armani T-shirt in here. Armani!

AYUB: Oh wow, thank God. My clothes are so ... thank you. If you just show me what to wear tonight, I will –

QADIR BHAI: Tonight?

AYUB: Yes, I don't have any ... I mean, all my clothes are so ... that's why you got this?

QADIR BHAI: How does it matter what you wear? You will be in the kitchen. You will be covered in spices and sauces, anyway. And before they enter, you will leave. Don't worry about clothes. I need your skill, Ayub. That's what I need. Your magic.

AYUB: Yes, of course. I meant ... I mean, in my head, I was excited, you know. Just happy for Javed. That's all.

QADIR BHAI: Good, good. (*giving AYUB money*) Here's some money. Get all the groceries you need.

*QADIR BHAI nudges AYUB towards the stairs,
the small door.*

Get some fresh mint as well. We'll start with some chai. Straight from Gerrard Street! I mean, Darjeeling! Wink, wink!

AYUB: Straight from Darjeeling ...

QADIR BHAI: And get some groceries for yourself as well. Whatever you need, okay? Stock up for the week. And cook extra tonight. You can bring some food back with you and eat a nice meal. Here, with Fatima. Call her and have an intimate meal.

AYUB: I will ...

QADIR BHAI can sense that AYUB feels injured.

QADIR BHAI: All this talk about what to wear. Why'd you bring that up? First, my wife. Then you. She wants to buy an outfit now. I'll have to drive her to a mall. Don't get me wrong. I don't mind. Not for a second. Just as Fatima is to you, my wife is to me. You just need that one person by your side, that's all.

AYUB: Oh, I would give anything to bring Fatima here. I promised
her that I would –

QADIR BHAI: Then work hard, Ayub. Work hard. Don't lose focus.

AYUB: I won't, I'll –

   QADIR BHAI sees the carpet near the door.

QADIR BHAI: What's that?

AYUB: Oh. It's nothing. It's a carpet.

QADIR BHAI: I know it's a carpet.

   He unrolls it.

Smooth. Very smooth.

AYUB: Is it? I …

QADIR BHAI: Must be expensive. Where'd you get it?

AYUB: Nowhere. I didn't buy it or anything.

QADIR BHAI: I hope not. You should be saving.

AYUB: Every dollar I make … it's in your hands for safekeeping.
I haven't bought a thing for myself since I got here. It's been
a while since I sent some money home. Without my passport,
they don't allow me –

QADIR BHAI: Good, good. Keep saving, keep saving.

AYUB: I do. I will.

QADIR BHAI: But you haven't answered my question.

AYUB: The carpet? Someone gave it to me.

QADIR BHAI: Who?

AYUB: A customer.

QADIR BHAI: A customer?

AYUB: Well, he's not exactly a customer. He's a taxi driver. I mean, he drives a cab for a living.

QADIR BHAI: Okay ...

AYUB: He gave it to me. As a gift.

QADIR BHAI: What did you do for him?

AYUB: Nothing. I didn't do anything.

QADIR BHAI: You didn't do anything.

AYUB: No ... nothing, really.

QADIR BHAI: And yet he gave you a gift. That too a carpet. You don't give a gift to someone just like that, do you?

AYUB: No ... I guess not.

QADIR BHAI: So what did you do for him then?

AYUB: I ... I just gave him food one night. After the place was closed.

QADIR BHAI: You gave food to a customer after closing?

AYUB: He wasn't a customer. Just someone in need of food.

QADIR BHAI: That's a customer.

AYUB: At first I refused, but he wouldn't take no for an answer. So I just gave him the food.

QADIR BHAI: Did he pay for it?

AYUB: No, no, I didn't take it. The register was closed.

QADIR BHAI: So you didn't take any money.

AYUB: Yes, I promise. You have my word.

QADIR BHAI: But ... he gave you a carpet. In exchange for one meal?

AYUB: Not one. Two. Just two meals.

QADIR BHAI: So you're taking favours in exchange for food?

AYUB: No, no, it's not that way at all. I just *gave* him the food.

QADIR BHAI: But it's not your food. It's the restaurant's food.

AYUB: I know, I ... I gave it to him one human being to another. It was late at night. It was dark.

QADIR BHAI: Dark? What has the dark go to do with anything?

AYUB: I'm just trying to explain. He came out of nowhere, and I hadn't spoken to anyone in so long. I hide in my room all day.

QADIR BHAI: You're meant to hide, Ayub. That was the deal. Or do you not remember?

AYUB: I do. I'm hiding.

QADIR BHAI: By exposing yourself to a stranger?

AYUB: I'm sorry, it was a mistake.

QADIR BHAI: It's an expensive carpet.

AYUB: Is it? I don't know ... I didn't know. I don't know much about carpets.

QADIR BHAI: All I'm saying is that it's expensive.

AYUB: I'll give it back. I don't want it.

QADIR BHAI: You don't want it?

AYUB: No. I never did. He –

QADIR BHAI: If you don't want it, give it away.

AYUB: I will. I'll just give it back to him.

QADIR BHAI: That would be an insult. To return a gift.

AYUB: Yes, perhaps you're right.

QADIR BHAI: May I suggest something?

AYUB: Of course, of course.

QADIR BHAI: Why not give it to me?

AYUB: To you?

QADIR BHAI: Not to *me*. I will find a place for it. I'm thinking of Mr. and Mrs. Smith. When they come over tonight, wouldn't it be wonderful for them to return home with a carpet?

AYUB: Yes ...

QADIR BHAI: Not with a carpet. *On* a carpet. I will say to them, "Leave your car here." And they will ask, "But how will we get home?" And I will present them with this beautiful carpet from ... where did you say it was from?

AYUB: I ... I don't know.

QADIR BHAI: This man, where is he from?

AYUB: Kashmir.

QADIR BHAI: Kashmir ... it's a Mughal carpet, Ayub. A Mughal carpet, you see? This is meant to be. What does this inscription say, do you know?

AYUB: No ... I didn't even see it properly.

QADIR BHAI: Ah, who cares? What will the Smiths know? For them it's straight out of the *Arabian Nights*. They will come in as Mr. and Mrs. Smith, and they will leave as two lovers in a fairy tale.

AYUB: I ... I can't.

QADIR BHAI: You can't what?

AYUB: I can't give it to you. I should return it to him.

QADIR BHAI: Why?

AYUB: I ... I just have to.

QADIR BHAI: That's what I thought.

AYUB: Qadir Bhai, please. Let me explain.

QADIR BHAI: I think I understand what's going on here. Not completely. But –

AYUB: There's nothing going on.

QADIR BHAI: Do you really think I would take your carpet?

AYUB: It's not mine. I don't want it. This man is strange. Ever since he's –

QADIR BHAI: Just be at the house by three.

AYUB: I will.

QADIR BHAI: And make sure you get the bill.

AYUB: What bill?

QADIR BHAI: For the groceries. Just make sure you get the bill.

AYUB: I always do. I always get the bill.

QADIR BHAI: Just reminding you.

> QADIR BHAI walks to the exit. Then he stops, looks at the tiles.

The tiles, Ayub.

AYUB: Yes, Qadir Bhai.

QADIR BHAI: In case Mr. and Mrs. Smith want to see the restaurant.

AYUB: Yes, yes, sure.

QADIR BHAI: The tiles.

QADIR BHAI exits.

AYUB gets down on his hands and knees. He starts scrubbing. Harder and harder. Like one possessed. By anger, by shame, who knows what else? If the floor had any flesh, AYUB would have reached the bone.

SCENE 2

A few hours later. AYUB is at the same spot, but in a deep sleep. JALAL enters the restaurant. He walks right up to AYUB. Stares at him. JALAL kneels down, wakes AYUB up. AYUB gets up with a start. He immediately moves away from JALAL. A horrible realization hits AYUB. He sits up in a huge panic.

AYUB: What time is it? Oh no ...

JALAL: Four o'clock.

AYUB: Oh no ... no ... what have I done?

He looks for his iPhone. The battery is dead.

It's dead.

AYUB rushes to the land line. Dials. He waits. No answer.

Oh God, please ...

JALAL: What's wrong?

AYUB: I have to be somewhere. I have to ...

JALAL: I can take you.

AYUB: No.

JALAL: I can take you. Aida will take you.

AYUB: Ever since you came here ...

AYUB rushes to the counter. Comes back with the carpet.

I don't want this.

JALAL: Why not?

AYUB: Please. Just take it back.

Just then, QADIR BHAI enters. He is fuming.

QADIR BHAI: What the hell is wrong with –

He realizes JALAL is present, but he is unable to control himself.

You were meant to be home an hour ago!

AYUB: I fell asleep. I –

QADIR BHAI: Don't lie to me. I called you.

AYUB: My battery is dead. See … please see for yourself.

QADIR BHAI: I called on the land line. It just rang and rang.

AYUB: I didn't hear a thing, I swear. I just fell asleep. Right here, I –

JALAL: He's not lying. I found him on the floor. Just a few moments ago.

QADIR BHAI ignores JALAL.

QADIR BHAI: Let's go.

AYUB: Yes, Qadir Bhai. Yes. I'm so sorry.

JALAL: Where are you taking him?

QADIR BHAI: Taking him? Who are you?

JALAL: It's a simple question.

QADIR BHAI: Who are you to question me? (*to AYUB*) Who is this?

JALAL: A friend.

QADIR BHAI: I'd like you to leave. We have to lock up.

JALAL: Where are you taking him?

QADIR BHAI: I don't have to answer you. (*to AYUB*) Who is this?

AYUB: (*to JALAL*) Please leave. Please, I beg you.

JALAL: Don't beg. Never beg.

AYUB: Just take your carpet and go. I'm … requesting you.

QADIR BHAI: Oh, this is your carpet. I see.

JALAL: See what?

QADIR BHAI: I don't have time for this, Ayub. We're already late.

AYUB: Yes, sir …

JALAL: "Sir?"

AYUB literally thrusts the carpet into JALAL's hands.

AYUB: Please.

AYUB follows QADIR BHAI. But JALAL blocks the entrance.

QADIR BHAI: What the hell are you doing?

JALAL: I just want to talk.

QADIR BHAI: About what?

JALAL: About Ayub.

QADIR BHAI: There's nothing to discuss.

JALAL: There might be.

QADIR BHAI: Get out of my way. Ayub, what is this?

   But JALAL doesn't budge.

   (*to JALAL*) Get out of my way before I –

JALAL: Before you what?

QADIR BHAI: Before I call the authorities!

JALAL: You mean the police.

QADIR BHAI: Yes, the police!

JALAL: Go ahead. Call the police. Call the authorities.

QADIR BHAI: (*to AYUB*) Who is this man?

AYUB: No one. He's –

JALAL: (*to AYUB*) A friend. I mean no harm.

QADIR BHAI: (*to AYUB*) What are you up to?

AYUB: Nothing, I'm not –

JALAL: I saw the mattress.

QADIR BHAI stiffens up a bit.

QADIR BHAI: Ayub, what's going on here?

JALAL: Talk to me, not him.

QADIR BHAI: (*to AYUB*) Is this how you repay my kindness?

AYUB: (*to JALAL*) Please, you'll get me in trouble. Please.

JALAL: Don't beg. Never beg.

QADIR BHAI: (*to AYUB*) You can stay here. I don't need you tonight. It's fine.

AYUB: What ... no, please. This is a misunderstanding. This is all –

QADIR BHAI: Better you stay here. I don't want snakes in my home.

AYUB: What? No ...

QADIR BHAI leaves.

Qadir Bhai, please!

JALAL: Don't beg. Never beg.

AYUB runs after QADIR BHAI.

AYUB: (*reaching into his pocket*) Bhai, the grocery money ... Bhai, please. At least take ...

But QADIR BHAI has left.

JALAL: I said don't beg.

AYUB: What have you done?

JALAL: Begging never convinces anyone.

AYUB: Do you even know what you've done?

JALAL: I just asked him a question.

AYUB: Who are you to ask questions?

JALAL: You are upset.

AYUB: Of course I'm ... what ...

> JALAL unrolls the carpet and places it on the ground.
> He smooths it out.

What are you doing?

JALAL: Jabeen made this carpet.

AYUB: Who?

JALAL: My wife, Jabeen.

AYUB: Your wife? You said you live alone.

JALAL: She's in Kashmir. Jabeen went back to Kashmir.

AYUB: I don't care. I have to –

JALAL: Come, pray with me.

AYUB: What?

JALAL: Let us pray.

AYUB: I don't want to pray. I need to –

JALAL: You need to pray so that you get strength. It's all making sense now. It's all … it's all butter chicken.

AYUB: You're mad. You are a madman.

JALAL gestures towards the carpet for AYUB to take his place.

JALAL: Please.

He gestures again. AYUB hesitates.

Never refuse an invitation for prayer.

AYUB kneels, reluctantly. JALAL remains standing. Then, after a few seconds, he starts circling AYUB.

AYUB: What are you doing?

JALAL: I drive a taxi for a living, but I'm an architect.

JALAL continues to circle AYUB as though he is inspecting him very closely. There is something ritualistic about the circling.

I used to be an architect.

AYUB's focus is on the circling.

AYUB: Why are you doing this?

JALAL: I smell something in you. You should know all about smell. You're a cook. You need to do something about that smell.

AYUB: What smell?

JALAL: You need to do something.

AYUB: Do what!

JALAL: Something. Anything.

>   *AYUB gets up.*

That tree ... I want you to look at it.

>   *AYUB stares at the tree outside.*

That is my tree. That night, that first night I came here, I had decided: I would drive Aida straight into that tree.

>   *AYUB looks at JALAL, surprised.*

I used to build mosques in Kashmir. Under my master's guidance. His mosques were like him: simple, humble.

After he died, my wife and I had an opportunity to move here. To this ... great land. At night, I drove a taxi. And the more I drove, the more I dreamed. My mosques would be big and magnificent.

That was my dream for this new land. Do you have dreams, Ayub? Everyone has dreams. We must confront our dreams.

The night we first met, I was sitting in the taxi, revving the engine ... waiting for the right moment. To let go, to accelerate. We lose sight of what's important because of our dreams. We become negligent. I was so desperate to build a mosque here, and I had met a man, the owner of all these taxis, a fellow Muslim, who would give me my first job as an architect.

On the night we were to finalize the deal, I took Aida with me to meet him. To show him how beautiful she ... that I am a family man ... that my mosques would be like ... we met at the taxi stand to sign the papers. I was giddy. Giddy with dreams. Of minarets and domes ...

I stepped out of my taxi ... my daughter was with me. Aida had insisted on coming along because I had promised her a late-night ride. She wanted to see why I was never home. What was I doing in these streets when everyone slept? When everyone was awake, why was I asleep? But Jabeen was against it. She said no, go alone. But I did not listen. I took Aida with me to meet this man, this semi-god, who, with a stroke of ink on paper, would make my dreams come true. Him signing his name across a dotted line was like ... like ... hariyae lekhit aao.[6]

And here we are at this taxi stand, where all the drivers are bowing to him, because I am not the only one with dreams. But that night, all eyes were on me. They knew I was this close to never driving a taxi again. I could feel their stares upon my skin, their question marks, their protests, their joy for me and their anguish for themselves. And as I listened to my overlord, to my fulfiller of dreams, I forgot myself. I was so giddy, so ... kenhti hyaki gasith[7]...

I saw my domes and minarets lighting the sky. ... and in that great imagining, and becoming One with my dream ... I forgot Aida. One minute she was next to me, the next minute, I saw her run ... from the corner of my eye ... it was as though she saw something. What did she see?

To this day, what did she see? Or was she running away from ... from *me*? And then, a sound. A thud. A simple thud. So recognizable to one who drives. The hood of a car, the hood

---

6   Kashmiri: Calligraphy from the heavens.

7   Kashmiri: Anything can happen.

hitting something, and then – stillness. I become giddy all over again. This time with dread. A dread I hope you never come to know. By the time Jabeen comes to the hospital, Aida has flown. She has flown, but she is still in my arms ...

... and I offer Aida to my wife ... the most shameless offering ...

JALAL mimes holding Aida's body in his arms like an offering.

... the most hideous gesture a man can make to his wife: here ... and she moves away from me. Jabeen cracks. I see her spine crack in front of my eyes ...

JALAL mimes snapping Jabeen's spine.

... like a twig from that tree ...

He snaps her spine again and again in great anguish.

... she never speaks to me again. She just sits at home all day and keeps weaving. Weaving and weeping, weeping and weaving ...

JALAL repeats the Arabic quote.

Lqd trknā klw šī' wara'ana, wa-madayna; fmā kān muqaddaran lnā, qd taḥaqqaqa. Lqd intahaynā, wa-ṣārat a'mālnā ḥikāyāt tuḥkā li-l-aṭfāl.[8]

At night, I beg Aida to come back to life. Don't beg, Ayub. Begging never works. So I tell Jabeen, "Yes, I am the one who did it. Okay? It's my fault. But try and understand. I saw it happen. I ... I carried my dead child in my arms!" She looks at me and says, "I

---

8   Arabic: We left it all behind, and off we went; what was fated, came to pass. We were done, and our doings became tales for the children.

understand," in the most gentle way. She nods, in the most gentle way, the way only Jabeen can. "You carried her dead in your arms. But I carried her alive, in my womb."

JALAL stays frozen – broken – as though he is hearing the truth of Jabeen's words all over again.

The next day, she goes back to Kashmir and leaves me crawling these streets at night. Until one night I can take no more. It is Aida's birthday, her first birthday after her death. I stop and stare at that tree. That tree with its thick, solid trunk.

JALAL and AYUB both stare at the tree. JALAL mimes he is in his taxi looking death in the face. He has his foot on the accelerator, his hand on the wheel, and he is revving the engine.

"Aida, what does your death mean? Please, I beg you."

JALAL mimes accelerating some more. His eyes fixed on the tree, about to meet his Maker.

"My flesh and blood, my love ... my heart outside of my heart ...

... you *will* show me." And then I see your light. Through that tree, the light of the moon. The Mughlai Moon. "Butter chicken," she says. "Don't we always eat butter chicken on my birthday?"

JALAL moves towards AYUB, corners him.

You see, I am the one who makes the trees shake ... I would have been. And that would have been the end of Aida. But I had already killed her once. I could not kill her again. The light in your restaurant saved me. The light in *you* saved me. Saved her. That is what I'm trying to say. You are a good man, Ayub. It's too late for me, but you ...

Negligence, Ayub. Don't you see? In my dreams and domes, there was negligence. You have a daughter back home. You are here.

AYUB: But ... what am I to do? What am I to do with ... what should I do?

JALAL: I cannot tell you what to do. But you must do something. Anything. Who haunts us when we are old? Who makes our teeth chatter? Who makes our stomach churn? Only our children can do that to us. Sirif panin shure.[9]

JALAL exits. AYUB is very displaced. He stares at the tree. The sound of the tree shaking in the wind. AYUB's hair starts moving, he feels the force of the wind, which is JALAL's words. He stands up, walks forward, but the wind is too strong. It is a gale now.

AYUB: Ghazal ...

AYUB reaches for his daughter.

Fatima ...

But the force of the gale is too strong. The more he tries, the more he is pushed back.

Until he is pushed back against the glass display case. Pinned against it like a puppet. He looks up at the sky.

Ghazal ... Fatima ...

---

9   Kashmiri: Only our children.

SCENE 3

The next morning. AYUB is placing food in the display case. QADIR BHAI enters. AYUB immediately stands still almost like a soldier at attention.

AYUB: Good morning, Qadir Bhai.

QADIR BHAI: Good morning.

AYUB: Good morning, sir ...

An awkward silence.

How was the –

QADIR BHAI: Fine.

AYUB: I'm sorry. Maybe it was the wrong question to ask.

QADIR BHAI: You mean the dinner.

AYUB: Yes, I should not have brought it up. The mistake is mine. Forgive me.

QADIR BHAI: It's okay. You can ask about it. (*beat*) Go ahead.

AYUB: Sorry?

QADIR BHAI: Go ahead. Ask how it was.

AYUB: How was ... last night's dinner?

QADIR BHAI: It was fine. More than fine. We missed your food. But once in a while, my wife surprises me. It's not like your food, but what do the Smiths know? They loved it.

AYUB: That's good. And ... the girl?

QADIR BHAI: The girl ... that girl, Cindy Smith. What can I say? She is a blessing. Guess what she is doing? I mean, what is she studying? Law! She's going to be a lawyer. Can you imagine? Husband and wife, both lawyers.

AYUB: That's ... quite a combination.

QADIR BHAI: Yes, yes. It is. That's interesting. Why do you say that?

AYUB isn't sure what QADIR BHAI means.

Why do you say it that way?

AYUB: I just meant ... it's a powerful combination.

QADIR BHAI: Hmm. I like what you say. Powerful. It *is* a powerful combination. How strange. When I think about it, that's exactly what I felt last night. I was watching them, sitting across from me on the sofa, these three individuals – Bob and Sheryl and Cindy – and I look at my wife, and she's conversing with them as though they're long-lost neighbours, and Cindy is talking to me, and she asks me, "So, what should I call you?" For a second, I have no idea. No one's ever asked me that. I just smiled and changed the topic. But then, suddenly, in the middle of a completely unrelated conversation, I just said to her, "Call me Qadir Bhai." It came out of nowhere. And my wife looked at me, and so did Javed. And I said, "Yes, Bhai means brother, but so what?" In a way, we are experiencing a common brotherhood right now, are we not? Two very different cultures, very different religions, uniting through love. I could never do this in India. I could never tell my son's bride-to-be, "Call me Qadir Bhai." It's so freeing. But that freedom comes from power. I realized that I have the power, I had *earned* the power to do that. So, when you say "powerful," how strange. How ... innate your understanding

— 86 —

of things. Last night, I suddenly saw my grandchildren, these off-white babies, strewn all over the living room – all future lawyers. So who cares if she's not Muslim? She's a lawyer. Their children will be lawyers. And what is religion, if not law? And suddenly I felt even more powerful. You are a wise soul, Ayub. So ... I have decided to give you one more chance. I have decided, despite last night's events, to start all over again.

AYUB: Oh. I would very much like that, Qadir Bhai. I would very much like that.

QADIR BHAI: I'm doing it out of respect for your baba. He was like a father to me. May the Almighty grant him eternal peace.

AYUB: I made a mistake. It won't –

QADIR BHAI: We all make mistakes. In any case, it would be unwise of me to feel any ill will towards you at such an auspicious time in my life.

AYUB: Thank you.

QADIR BHAI: It is an auspicious time for you as well.

AYUB: Yes, it is. I'm sure it is.

QADIR BHAI: Ayub, you're going to Montréal.

AYUB: What?

QADIR BHAI: You are moving to Montréal. To start the new Mughlai Moon there.

AYUB: Oh, Qadir Bhai ...

QADIR BHAI: Now you believe? Now you are sure?

AYUB: Yes, yes! This is ...

QADIR BHAI: God's will. That's all it is.

AYUB: So my passport is ... my status is done?

QADIR BHAI: Your status?

AYUB: I'm a resident now?

QADIR BHAI: A resident? Well, no, not yet. That will take time.

AYUB: But then how –

QADIR BHAI: You will go *there*, just as you are *here* ... you will
be *there* what you are *here*. I mean, there is no real difference,
is there? Only difference is, this time you will train a cook there,
teach him all you know. Think of it as a cultural exchange.
It will be good for you. Maybe you'll pick up some French as
well. Oui. Petit. Bonjour! Say it. Say "bonjour."

AYUB: But ... when will I get my passport back?

QADIR BHAI: Your passport? Anytime. I can return your passport
to you anytime. It's your *status* that I'm working on.

AYUB: But it's been years ... it's been four years.

QADIR BHAI: Your situation is complex, Ayub. It's not cut and
dried. Look, why don't you ... here, why don't you talk to the
lawyer directly? Jacques, the French lawyer. He will explain.

AYUB: He's an immigration lawyer?

QADIR BHAI: He's the Mughlai Moon lawyer. Think of him as our
lawyer. Why don't you speak directly to him? Here –

QADIR BHAI dials.

AYUB: But what –

QADIR BHAI: (*into the phone*) Jacques, it's Qadir. The young man I was talking to you about, the one we're helping. Yes, I'm with him. Oh, he's eager, for sure, but I'd like to assure him, I'd like *you* to assure him, that we're looking after him. Here –

AYUB: No, no, it's okay.

QADIR BHAI: Speak with him. Speak with Jacques.

QADIR BHAI passes the phone to AYUB.

AYUB: Hello?

AYUB listens. A lot of nodding.

Yes, okay … I see … yes, okay … but –

He is cut off. More nodding.

Okay, bye.

QADIR BHAI: Say "bonjour."

AYUB: Okay, bonjour …

But by then QADIR BHAI has taken the phone away.

QADIR BHAI: I'll speak to you later, Jacques. Bonjour, bonjour. (*beat*) Oh, sorry. Salut! Yes, salut! (*to AYUB*) See – this is what I mean. I said hello instead of goodbye. It's too late for me. Maybe I can't learn. But your generation – the Javeds and Ayubs of this world – there is hope. Don't worry, he is tops. Jacques is tops.

He's like French cuisine. Delicate. He will take your delicate matter and give it his delicate touch. Just be patient …

What is it now? Don't think so much. It's a new start!

> *QADIR BHAI senses that AYUB has not been put at ease by his words.*

AYUB: I … can I go to India and come back?

> *QADIR BHAI comes closer to AYUB.*

QADIR BHAI: (*very fatherly*) Look, Ayub … certain sacrifices have to be made. To get something, you have to lose something. That's what migration does. It takes away. It takes away, and how.

Your job here is cushy compared to what I had to do. I was a lowly labourer. They wouldn't even talk to me, Ayub. They wouldn't even talk to me. I sat alone in the …

But look at me now. I have a home, a family … with these same labourer's hands, I will lift my grandchildren.

You think Allah would have given me all this if I didn't deserve it?

So be patient. Your home, your family, it will all come. But you have to pay your dues. Then you will belong here.

Today, I'm a Ka-*Deer*!

> *QADIR BHAI does an absurd light walk. His version of a nimble deer.*

Don't you want to feel like that? Beautiful? That's what Canada does.

AYUB: But then ... why do I feel so ugly?

QADIR BHAI senses that AYUB is still lacklustre. He takes some cleaning equipment. QADIR BHAI is on his hands and knees. Scrubbing.

What are you doing?

QADIR BHAI: I'm doing your job. To show you there is no shame in it. It's all in your hands. How you feel is in your hands.

AYUB: I will do it, Qadir Bhai.

AYUB takes the scrubber from QADIR BHAI.

QADIR BHAI: I don't want you to think I am too good for this work. Or this work is not good enough for me.

AYUB: Please. Let me.

QADIR BHAI: Are you sure? I want you to be okay, Ayub.

AYUB: I'm okay, I'm okay ...

QADIR BHAI: Okay, then. I will see you later.

AYUB starts cleaning.

(*as he's leaving*) We're all in this together ...

AYUB: No.

QADIR BHAI: What do you mean, no?

But AYUB is responding to something else. Out of nervousness and sheer confusion, he starts scrubbing the

tiles furiously. Then he stops, suddenly. Stares at the tiles.
He sees something. His own reflection. He is shocked.

AYUB: No ...

QADIR BHAI: What is it?

AYUB touches his face. He starts scrubbing the tiles even
more. Now, when he speaks, he addresses his own reflection.

AYUB: No ...

QADIR BHAI: What's wrong?

AYUB: Who do these people think they are?

QADIR BHAI: Who the hell are you talking to?

AYUB: He won't understand. He will *never* understand.

QADIR BHAI: Understand what?

AYUB: How many more leftovers will you eat? How long will
you hide?

QADIR BHAI: Understand what, Ayub?

AYUB: Our pain means nothing to him.

QADIR BHAI: What do you mean?

Now AYUB looks at QADIR BHAI.

AYUB: Never welcome. Always hiding. Always under the table.
Isn't that the expression? To work under the table?

QADIR BHAI: What? How can you say that?

AYUB: Am I wrong?

QADIR BHAI: You ungrateful ... I brought you to Canada. You were dying to get out of there. That was the deal. You agreed to it. I brought you to Canada.

AYUB: You brought me to a kitchen. I don't live in Canada. I live in a kitchen. But I must thank you. For making me clean the tiles. I have seen my face. I have seen who I am.

Look ... look at what you've done to me.

But QADIR BHAI can't see a thing.

The rat in the restaurant ...

QADIR BHAI: What rat?

AYUB: That rat is *me.*

QADIR BHAI: What rat?

AYUB: Now that I have seen my face, don't you want to see yours?

QADIR BHAI: How dare you!

AYUB: Maybe you are not a deer. Please, have a look. The tiles will show you.

QADIR BHAI: That's it. I'm done with you!

AYUB: Can you hear that, Qadir Bhai? Can you hear the rumbling underneath? I thought it was a subway at first, but now I know. Those are my brothers. There are hundreds of me, hiding. Underneath. Created by people like you. They are all over, Qadir Bhai. They are rumbling because their pain means nothing. But power, where does it come from? It comes from pain. My face, I can feel ...

AYUB touches his face again. He starts shaking his head, like a nervous twitch. He starts circling QADIR BHAI.

Maybe I should call immigration?

QADIR BHAI: Immigration? You want to call immigration? Call them. What do you think they'll do? I have a Canadian passport. I am a citizen of this country. I have a lawyer. All I get is a heavy fine. You think I don't know that? I knew that. I took the risk. For *you.*

AYUB: For me?

QADIR BHAI: Yes, for you. For your baba. For my old friend. Before he died, I made him a promise that I would get you out of the country.

AYUB: Don't talk about my baba. You have no right to speak his name.

QADIR BHAI: And now you want to be an informer?

AYUB: But isn't that what rats are?

AYUB starts forming teeth. Fangs. He starts chittering away like a rat.

QADIR BHAI: Your father would have been ashamed of you! You're a disgrace!

AYUB: *I'm* a disgrace?

AYUB moves towards QADIR BHAI.

I can see my face. My teeth, my whiskers. I can see how dirty I am. But I am ... I am also beautiful. This country runs on people like me, people who have been trampled on, I see myself in them, I see ... rats are beautiful. You experiment on them. You find cures because of them. They sacrifice their lives for the greater good, don't they? But are *you* the greater good?

AYUB grabs QADIR BHAI and pins him to the ground. QADIR BHAI resists but AYUB is too powerful. He now thrusts QADIR BHAI's face into the tiles.

Who is staring back at you? Tell me. The tiles are telling the truth, Qadir Bhai. If you can truly see yourself as the greater good, I will let you go.

See your face! Are you the greater good?

QADIR BHAI: (*struggling*) Let me go ... please ... Ayub ... let me ...

AYUB: I have nothing ... these winters ... that cold, dark sky, it is my future, the lie I told Fatima, the lie you sold me ... it's the winters ... there's no sun here, what kind of place ... I have nothing to show, nothing to give my wife, my child.

What can I give them? What does a rat have to offer? What can I ...

In a fit of madness, AYUB bites QADIR BHAI on the cheek. QADIR BHAI screams in pain. The scream jolts AYUB out of his raging trance. He lets go of QADIR BHAI, stunned by what he has just done. QADIR BHAI scampers away and leaves the restaurant. AYUB sits in silence, trying to make sense of what has just happened.

SCENE 4

A couple of days later. JALAL and AYUB are seated at a table like two friends. AYUB has a packed suitcase. The carpet is rolled up next to the suitcase.

AYUB: I wish I had something to show for my time here. All I have are my savings. At least he gave me that. Said he was doing right by Allah.

JALAL: Money isn't ... Paison ne mere aur Jabeen ke liye kya kiya?[10]

AYUB: (*responding in Urdu for the first time*) Bas ... kuch bhi ho ... ki mein Canadian hona mehsoos kar sakoon.[11] A real Canadian, you know? Like being able to call Fido. I want to feel that.

JALAL: Fido?

AYUB: Yes, just call Fido. Get my own number, ask for a better deal or I will go to Rogers. Or just sit at Starbucks and order a coffee under my name, and when they call out my name, Ayub! – not feel like a thief. Or if I am sick, a prescription in my name ... that recognizes I am unwell, that acknowledges my body ... that I am in pain ... I don't want my heart to pound each time a customer enters the restaurant ... I want to be able to introduce myself as ... *myself* ... without fear ...

Beat.

JALAL: On the other hand, at least your commute to work was short.

---

10 Urdu: What good did money do for me and Jabeen?

11 Urdu: Just ... something ... that makes me feel like a Canadian.

AYUB: That's true. The shortest commute in the history of commutes.

> *AYUB and JALAL chuckle. But the gloom comes back.*

What do I tell my daughter? That for four years I hid in the basement of a restaurant?

JALAL: You did not hide.

> *But AYUB is not convinced.*

Tell your daughter you lived. But not in the basement.

AYUB: I can't lie. I'm tired of lying.

JALAL: You're not lying. You're just making a small adjustment. What if you told her you lived *behind* the restaurant? Behind the moon ...

AYUB: What?

JALAL: The Mughlai Moon ...

AYUB: Ah ...

JALAL: Now that's not a bad place to live, is it? (*beat*) People have landed on the moon. You have lived behind it.

AYUB: All I know is ... I was a fool to come here. A fool came. A fool went.

> *Beat.*

JALAL: Show me your passport.

AYUB: What?

JALAL: Just show me.

AYUB does.

You look older now.

AYUB: Thank you so much. That really boosts my confidence. I'll be reuniting with my wife, who looks better than ever. So now I'm older and still poor. Nice going, Brother.

JALAL: What's the difference between this man in the photograph and this man before me?

AYUB: Apparently, you already gave me the answer.

JALAL: I'm serious, Ayub.

AYUB: I don't know.

JALAL: This is a man who left his wife and child. This is a man who is returning to them.

AYUB: A man who failed to get them into this country ... Canada will never happen for them now ...

JALAL: So what?

AYUB: It means I failed. I'm a failure.

> *But JALAL senses that AYUB still hasn't understood what he is trying to say.*

JALAL: At least you have them. When you return home, you get to hug your daughter. You get to hold on to her for as long as you like. (*beat*) We had her late ... and she left so early ...

AYUB takes in JALAL's pain. He understands. But he still doesn't know what to say in response.

AYUB: Why don't you go back as well? Me to Mumbai. You to Kashmir.

JALAL: I can't.

AYUB: Why not?

JALAL: Because of Jabeen. She told me to stay here. She told me I should stay.

Beat. AYUB gets up from his chair and unrolls the carpet.

AYUB: Come, sit ...

JALAL: No, we should get going ...

AYUB: Sit. Trust me. You do trust me, don't you?

JALAL nods. AYUB kneels. AYUB pats the ground, a signal for JALAL to join him.

Please.

JALAL does.

Above us, a dome, the most beautiful dome. A dome that is the most truthful dome, because life itself is a circle ...

Minarets, our pillars of truth, our pillars of righteousness. May we always speak the truth. May we always defend the truth. May we stand tall and erect, like the truth.

May Jabeen rise again, like a minaret. May her broken back mend itself and be strong like a minaret.

May Aida rise again. May Jabeen rise again.

JALAL: Canada gifted us a child. And my greed took it away. Why couldn't I just drive a taxi?

AYUB: We will build a mosque. Just like you wanted. Your gift to the Almighty.

It's your turn. Build it with me.

> *JALAL is thinking. But he's not there yet. AYUB senses this.*

Start with one thing. Anything.

What do you see?

JALAL: I can't … I …

AYUB: Close your eyes. Let us close our eyes.

> *AYUB closes his eyes, places his hands in his lap.*
> *So does JALAL.*

Now tell me what you see.

JALAL: I … I see the minarets.

AYUB: That's good. Stay with the minarets. Are they tall or short?

JALAL: They are tall. So tall …

AYUB: What else …

JALAL: I …

AYUB: They're right before you, Brother. Can you see Jabeen? Allow yourself to see her …

JALAL: Jabeen ... Jabeen ...

JALAL calls her name with love and longing.

Jabeen ...

*His voice is tinged with pain and regret. AYUB feels this.
He counters it.*

AYUB: She is climbing the minaret. She is so graceful and with
such clear purpose. She is now atop one minaret ...

AYUB waits for JALAL to continue.

JALAL: And at the other end is Fatima ... she is atop the other ...
and they are the muezzin, my brother, together they call
for us ...

AYUB: They are the real muezzin ...

Now JALAL is gathering confidence and momentum.

JALAL: And they shall lead us in prayer tonight ... and from this
moment on, I hear their voices call us, calm us, comfort us ...

Now JALAL is unstoppable, electric.

For they are the ones who shall carry us. Yes, pain has brought
us to our knees, but they are telling us to start again, they are
telling us to dream again. They are calling for a new beginning.

JALAL lets out a beautiful, mournful cry.

La-i-la-ha-íl-lal-lah; Mu-ham-ma-dur-ra-su-lul-lah![12]

---

12 Arabic: There is no god but God and Muhammad is the messenger of God.

AYUB: La-i-la-ha-íl-lal-lah; Mu-ham-ma-dur-ra-su-lul-lah.

JALAL: La-i-la-ha-íl-lal-lah; Mu-ham-ma-dur-ra-su-lul-lah.

AYUB: La-i-la-ha-íl-lal-lah; Mu-ham-ma-dur-ra-su-lul-lah.

JALAL: La-i-la-ha-íl-lal-lah; Mu-ham-ma-dur-ra-su-lul-lah.

JALAL and AYUB: La-i-la-ha-íl-lal-lah;
Mu-ham-ma-dur-ra-su-lul-lah.

La-i-la-ha-íl-lal-lah; Mu-ham-ma-dur-ra-su-lul-lah.

> *JALAL and AYUB repeat this line together, again and again, as they ask for forgiveness. They bring the crescendo down to a beautiful, haunting whisper.*

> *Then, we sit with them in silence, for a very brief moment, their eyes closed, knowing that one journey is done, but another is about to begin.*

> *The end*

AFTERWORD

When the fluorescent lights flicker on at 3 a.m., the buzz of the Mughlai Moon immediately provokes a sense of familiarity. We've flocked before to this restaurant in the late hours of the night, we've savoured the spices that soak in behind the display case, and we can almost smell the hours of preparation put into the rich butter chicken. It's when we hear the squeaks of glass cleaning that we discover the Moon's devoted inhabitant, Ayub, and the realization sparks that this is not just a place we recognize, it is a safe haven for a man who has risked his life and spirit to find new ground.

What is most exquisite about Anosh Irani's ability to translate this story of connection and disconnection isn't simply his unpacking of the system in which hundreds of people seek refuge or are looking for paths towards an illusion of freedom. It is his deep dive into the psychological impact of what that seeking entails. Ayub, in all his yearning, is equally tortured by his environment, where the buzzing of lights and kitchen appliances blends into the sounds within the walls, in the nooks and crannies of the restaurant, accompanied by chattering rodent teeth – the vermin of society. The Mughlai Moon is not entirely safe; it is a manifested cage that only magnifies the trap in Ayub's mind.

I had the great pleasure of reading an earlier draft of *Behind the Moon* during my transition into artistic director of Tarragon Theatre – the play was commissioned by previous AD Richard Rose. I was fortunate to have the opportunity to follow through with Anosh's offering in my first season. As one would hope in any enriched new play development process, Anosh had an eagerness to respond to what the story was asking of him and how the relationships between these men act as a microcosm of the intense (and often silent) realities of immigration to Canada. But the story is more than that; it asks us to investigate what community means. It challenges us to examine our demons and how we connect to them for worse or for the possibility of release.

The resonance of this script and its first production at Tarragon was profound. At a time when bridging audiences back to live performance post-pandemic presented challenges, *Behind the Moon* captivated us and invited us meaningfully all together back to the theatre. Moreover, while we continued to expand the scope of Canadian identity through our mission, our plays, and their storytellers, *Behind the Moon* coupled beauty in form with an urgency to make audiences look beyond and behind the people or places that offer a sense of familiarity, in the hopes of deeper connection. Triumphantly, Anosh reminds us of the complex humanity behind the stories that we may not be exposed to or choose to distance ourselves from.

Like a gust of wind bursting open the door, it can take an unexpected force for change to happen in ourselves.

Ultimately, *Behind the Moon* places a mirror within us through Ayub, Jalal, and Qadir Bhai who – whether they or we desire it or not – may be stronger when they are woken up from what they have left behind (or what we hold onto) in order to survive tomorrow.

—MIKE PAYETTE

Artistic Director, Tarragon Theatre

INTERVIEW
WITH ANOSH IRANI

What was the genesis of Behind the Moon? *It sounds like it evolved in several phases.*

In 2018 the Arts Club Theatre Company premiered my play *The Men in White*. It's a story about two brothers, Abdul and Hasan, and their bond with each other, explored via their shared passion for cricket. Abdul works under the table in an Indian restaurant in Vancouver and plays under a false name for a ragtag cricket team. Tired of losing, the team decides to bring Hasan – an ace cricketer – over from Mumbai for one summer. That's the premise of the play. It deals with brotherhood, immigration, and Islamophobia.

But long after the play was done, Abdul continued to haunt me.

There is one monologue in the play where he talks about how, when immigration officers show up at the restaurant where he works, he sits down at the nearest table and pretends to be a customer. But he's so panicked that he does not realize he's chewing on chicken bones that the previous customer had left on their plate. This image, and his fear and humiliation, stayed with me. When a character refuses to leave, it's a sign that their internal world needs more interrogation.

But I had already written a play.

However, at the time I was working on a collection of short stories.

I had this image of Abdul living in the basement of the restaurant (The Mughlai Moon), in a tiny windowless room, chasing a rat. He was so lonely that he was almost grateful for the rat. The location changed to Toronto because he was freezing, his teeth chattering. So I wrote a short story called "Behind the Moon," which allowed me to get closer to this version of Abdul's character. The story was published in the *Los Angeles Review of Books*, and eventually in my collection *Translated from the Gibberish: Seven Stories and One Half Truth*.

I was finally done with Abdul. But he was not done with me.

When I was in Toronto for a reading of my book, I had lunch in an Indian restaurant. There were a few parked taxis outside, and I remember this tree moving in the wind. It's possible that the tree did not exist, I don't know. But here was this fictional character again, feeling more real than ever, spraying cleaning liquid on the glass case that displays the food. And when I looked at the taxis outside, I thought, "Someone needs to come in and apply pressure on Abdul. I need to see him crack completely." In walks a taxi driver at 3 a.m., asking for Indian food even though the restaurant is closed. And I had no idea if his intentions were good or suspect. So I had to look into his internal life as well.

And thus began the theatrical version of *Behind the Moon*.

I changed Abdul's name to Ayub, and I literally felt his yearning to be with his wife and daughter again. They were in Mumbai, and it had been four years since he had seen them. For that he needed permission from the owner of the restaurant, Qadir Bhai. The triumvirate was now complete. Caught between the taxi driver's mysterious web and the owner's kind but manipulative behaviour, Ayub unravels, spiralling completely out of control. I ended up weaving a story about three Muslim men, all from Mumbai, who had moved to Canada. It's an immigration story, no doubt, which made me realize that no two immigrant journeys are alike.

When I write a character, I always ask them, "How are you wounded?" And I listen to their pain. It is their pain that haunts me and refuses to leave. In the end, as a playwright and as a human being, I believe in the power of deep listening. If you can truly listen to what a character has been though, without any moral judgement, you will find depth in the work. I listened to these three men, all of whom were in pain, and their dreams and desires fuelled this work.

Thank you for this beautiful answer. As you say, Behind the Moon *is an immigration story that points to the reality that there is no single immigration story. Even if the play's three characters are all caught up in the same shared economic and political conditions, their narratives are very different and yet connected by the question of what success looks like for them. Can we ask you about Qadir Bhai, the most obviously "successful" of these men? You mention his "kind but manipulative behaviour." He clearly exploits Ayub's situation for his own gain, but he also seems at least partially to believe in his own sincerity – "I understand your need, Ayub"* – and in attempting to relate to Ayub and reassure *him, Qadir Bhai makes a point of referring to his own struggles: "I am a small man who came from nothing, and I am now a Monsieur … I come from nothing, Ayub" (scene 4).*

You say, "When I write a character, I always ask them, 'How are you wounded?'" Qadir Bhai's particular pain seems to be clouding his ability to ask this same question of Ayub. Is his wound that he can't see himself clearly?

That's the effect of his wound. Qadir's Bhai's wound is that because he went through humiliation and isolation, he feels it's a rite of passage, a requirement for Ayub as well. Part of it is false justification, but somewhere he also believes he is right. "I had to go through hell to get to where I am," is what he thinks, "so why shouldn't you?" It made him stronger, more determined. In his mind, the humiliation and hardship led to success. He applies that same thinking when it comes to his own son. He spoils Javed, but when Ayub tells Qadir Bhai to "trust Javed," Qadir Bhai responds: "Trust Javed? That's interesting. I mean sure, he's my son, but he's also … an idiot. He's been through nothing. Can you trust someone who's been through nothing?" So this has become part of his worldview. However, he also knows that he is taking advantage of Ayub. The sad part is he finds ways to justify this. So you're right – he cannot see himself clearly. And at the end of the play, Ayub does him that favour. Ayub shows Qadir Bhai who he truly is. It's ironic that Qadir Bhai insists that Ayub keep the tiles spotless: "I need to see my face, Ayub." When Qadir Bhai's blindness reaches its zenith, the tiles are ready to reflect the truth.

So in the end Ayub offers Qadir Bhai the gift of truth. It's the culmination of a number of gifts –the giving of food, the used iPhone, the carpet, the garbage/clothes, even the "gift" of Aida ("Canada gifted us a child"). And as Jalal says, "Not all gifts are the same." Some of them are considerably more generous and more welcome than others; in fact in Behind the Moon *they seem to have disparate functions for giver and receiver. Can you talk a bit about the role of gift-giving in the play?*

There are some things that come out of nowhere. The carpet was one such discovery. I had no idea where it came from. But suddenly Jalal had this "gift" for Ayub. And I thought to myself, "What's he doing? What is he carrying?" When Jalal revealed the carpet, I just followed the clues. Characters end up giving us hints. It's up to us, as writers, to follow their lead. When Jalal unravels the gift, it contains a warning. It feels that way to Ayub. This is because the previous "gift" – the used iPhone given to him by Qadir Bhai – felt like a betrayal. It hurt him. So he is now wary of receiving another gift.

Generally, in life, when we unwrap gifts, we do so with excitement and anticipation. Sometimes, because of that, we can also get disappointed: a terrible sweater, a book you'd never read, a coffee mug with an ugly image on it. But that's where it ends. In this play, however, the gifts have far-reaching consequences. The gifts incite an unravelling. The quotation on the carpet contains a warning of sorts. Then, when Qadir Bhai sees the carpet, that same "gift" gets Ayub into more trouble. But in the end, the carpet brings them together and allows them the possibility of forgiving themselves.

It's all about interpretation. How we interpret the events in our lives is so important. We have the power to transform things – both in a positive way and in a way that leads us into further darkness. The true gift is the wisdom to interpret what happens to us.

"The gifts incite an unravelling" is a wonderfully evocative line. It makes us wonder about what in the play might incite a piecing back together or healing. One road to healing that the play suggests has to do with the role of women in these men's lives. The play ends with the imagined figures of Jabeen and Fatima assuming extraordinary powers and becoming "the real muezzin," calling Ayub and Jalal to healing and "a new beginning." At the same time, women are physically absent from the play, only present as avatars in Ayub and Jalal's imaginations. How do women function in this unravelling-that-leads-to-the-possibility-of-forgiveness?

I wanted the presence of these two women to be felt throughout the play in the same way the characters – their husbands – experience their presence: through absence. The physical distance is an obvious reason for them feeling the absence of their wives. Fatima and Jabeen are back in India. However, the other, more palpable, absence is due to the guilt that these two men feel. They have pushed the women away because of what they have done or failed to do. When Ayub and Jalal both look back, they realize that their wives had given them some kind of warning. For instance, Jabeen had told Jalal *not* to take Aida with him to meet the architect, his "fulfiller of dreams." But Jalal did not listen. Ayub moved to Canada to provide for his wife and child and eventually bring them "here." But that was his own desire, his own want. Fatima did not ask him to do that. So both men acted on their own impulses and now must face the consequences of their actions. In their minds, the women were wiser and are therefore the real muezzin. It may or may not be true, but their guilt and their strong need for forgiveness have caused this distortion. Or true vision, who knows? Both men came to Canada in search of "a better life." And this is one of the questions I began the play with. We so often hear people say, "I came here in search of a better life." But what does that mean? And is this life that immigrants fall into really better? If it is not, the decision to move "here," wherever that may have been, becomes a regret, and unfortunately, in some cases, extremely painful. Therefore the need for forgiveness comes in. At some point, the pain is so intense that the only healing on offer is self-healing. And it begins with forgiveness.

Thank you, Anosh.

Questions by Catriona Strang and Ryan Fitzpatrick

ACKNOWLEDGMENTS

The playwright is extremely grateful to the following individuals for their help during the development of this play: David Adams, Henna Amin, Lois Anderson, Sohail Ansari, Raoul Bhaneja, Rachel Ditor, Rawi Hage, Faisal Hawa, Nazanine Hozar, Boman Irani, Cameron Johnston, Sam Kalilieh, Ali Kazmi, Nadeem Phillip Umar Khitab, Kayvon Khoshkam, Husein Madhavji, Justin Miller, Leora Morris, Maryam Najafi, Myekah Payne, Vik Sahay, May Seigneurie, Jai Singh, Ivan Smith, Meghan Speakman, Deivan Steele, Nidhi Tulli, and Pam Winter.

My deepest gratitude to Richard Rose for commissioning this play, for his insightful notes, and for a fantastic premiere production. To Mike Payette and Andrea Vagianos for their guidance and support; the fabulous cast, crew, and design team for their inspiring work; everyone at Talonbooks for this beautiful edition, especially Kevin Williams for publishing this play, Catriona Strang for her patience and her thoughtful edits, and Leslie Smith for an excellent cover; and the Canada Council for the Arts for generous financial assistance during the writing of this play.

Jalal's quote in English is from an epigraph to a short story titled "Interregnum" by Naiyer Masud published by Penguin Random House of India in Masud's *Collected Stories*. The original Farsi quote is from the tenth century Persian poet Kisa'i Marvazi. English translation by Muhammad Umar Memon. Arabic translation by Ahmed Moneka and Israa Moneka.

Talonbooks would like to thank Rahat Kurd, Hina Mahajan, Farhat Rehman, Norah Alkharashi, and Shevan Youssef for their assistance with language checks and transliterations.

Behind The Moon was originally commissioned by Tarragon Theatre, Richard Rose, Artistic Director. The play was staged by arrangement with Pam Winter, GGA, www.ggagency.ca.

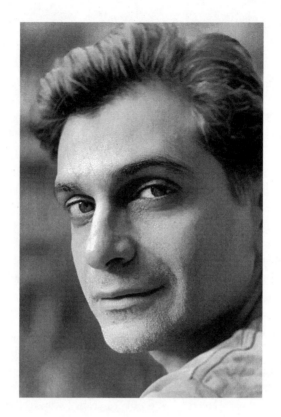

Photo: Boman Irani

Anosh Irani has published four critically acclaimed novels: *The Cripple and His Talismans* (2004), a national bestseller; *The Song of Kahunsha* (2006), which was an international bestseller and shortlisted for Canada Reads and the Ethel Wilson Fiction Prize; *Dahanu Road* (2010), which was longlisted for the Man Asian Literary Prize; and *The Parcel* (2016), which was a finalist for the Governor General's Literary Award for Fiction and the Writers' Trust Fiction Prize. His play *Bombay Black* (2006) won the Dora Mavor Moore Award for Outstanding New Play, as did his one-man show *Buffoon* (2019). His anthology *The Bombay Plays: The Matka King & Bombay Black* (2007) and his play *The Men in White* (2018) were both finalists for the Governor General's Literary Award for Drama, and in 2023 Irani was the recipient of the Writers' Trust Engel Findley Award. *Behind the Moon* was a finalist for the Dora Mavor Moore Award for Outstanding New Play. Irani's short stories have appeared in *Granta* and the *Los Angeles Review of Books* and have been collected in *Translated from the Gibberish: Seven Stories and One Half Truth* (2019). His nonfiction has been published in the *Globe and Mail*, the *Toronto Star*, the *Guardian*, and the *New York Times*. His work has been translated into eleven languages, and he teaches fiction and playwriting in the School of Creative Writing at the University of British Columbia.